ESAU JONES
BOUNTY HUNTER

OTHER BOOKS BY JIM FEAZELL

"COME THE SWINE"
A SUPERNATURAL THRILLER

"DRY HEAT"
A POLICE DRAMA

"THE LORD'S SHARE"
A LOVE TO KILL FOR

Dual Novelettes
"THE LEGEND OF CAT MOUNTAIN"
A SUPERNATURAL MYSTERY
and
"THE TROUBLE WITH RODNEY"
A SUPERNATURE MYSTERY

"RETURN TO HEAVEN"
A SUPERNATURAL THRILLER

"MAMA'S PLACE"
A REDNECK CHRONICLE

"JESSE"
A SUPERNATURAL THRILLER

Available from iuniverse.com
via www.jimfeazell.com

ESAU JONES

BOUNTY HUNTER

An
Irregular Love Story

BY

JIM FEAZELL

iUniverse, Inc.
Bloomington

ESAU JONES Bounty Hunter
An Irregular Love Story

iUniverse books may be ordered through booksellers or by contacting:

iUniverse
1663 Liberty Drive
Bloomington, IN 47403
www.iuniverse.com
1-800-Authors (1-800-288-4677)

ISBN: 978-1-4620-1548-1 (sc)
ISBN: 978-1-4620-1547-4 (ebook)

Printed in the United States of America

iUniverse rev. date: 6/29/2011

For **Sherry...my love.**

Foreword

It was the spring of 1865, the war had ended, the president had been assassinated, reconstruction had began before the war ended and the border country of north and south was in a state of chaotic turmoil.

Factions from both sides of the war had their lives up-heaved and destroyed beyond any normal repair. Esau Jones was one of such men. He was only a sixteen year old boy when he rode as a renegade bushwhacker with William Quantrill causing havoc with Union sympathizers and Union troops in the Kansas and Missouri border country. He also rode with "Bloody Bill" Anderson during the infamous Lawrence, Kansas massacre. He was a friend of Jesse and Frank James during these horrendous and harrowing times. It was once said by Jesse that Esau was the fastest and most accurate shot with an Army Colt of any one he had ever seen. At one time he had said that a mounted group of redleg militia was riding toward them at breakneck speed and Esau, wielding two revolvers, dropped eight of them while I only got two.

During these tumultuous times in "Little Dixie", Guerrilla warfare still gripped the border country of Kansas and Missouri between secessionist "bushwhackers" and Union forces, which largely consisted of local militia organizations ("jayhawkers" and "redlegs"). Bitter conflicts ensued, bringing an escalating cycle of atrocities by both sides. Guerrillas murdered civilian Unionists, executed prisoners and scalped the dead. Union forces made up mostly of Redleg militia enforced martial law with raids on homes, arrest of civilians, summary executions and banishment of Confederate sympathizers from the border states. It was during this time near Esau's twentieth year that a group of redleg militia burned the Jones farm murdering his Father, his Mother and his young sister. Esau knew nothing of the brutal massacre of his family until two months afterward. So he did not know which actual group of redlegs committed the atrocity, but no matter,, to him they were all to blame.

The Union redleg militia's lost many a blue-belly redleg for the next two years, before Esau decided to leave and head West in search of some kind of honest employment and make a life for himself. Jesse James was getting over a life-threatening wound he received right at the end of the war. He tried to get Esau to stay and join him in banditry. Esau graciously refused saying he wished to go west.

For the next two years Esau drifted north from Kansas-City up to Omaha and back down to Lincoln through Indian territory and occasionally picking up an odd job to take care of his meager needs. Sometime he would light for a few weeks to break some horses or take up for awhile with a woman. He had come accustomed to killing every redleg he accidently ran across. So, sometimes when he wasn't ready to leave, he pulled up stakes because he had learned there were large numbers of redleg militia looking for him, with a large reward on his head for the man who brought him down, posted by non-governmental entities who dedicated themselves to riding society of all former Confederate bushwhackers which were still considered Confederate sympathizers. Due to his known personal vendetta against redlegs, Esau Jones was put on top of the list. So, it wasn't because he was afraid to stay and fight them. He just knew which side his bread was buttered on— and he was not ready to die. He would welcome a few, but not twenty or thirty at once. And he, as yet, had not found his calling.

Esau had at one time given considerable thought to joining the Texas Rangers, until he found out he would have to fight with a large regiment of Rangers, mostly controlling Mexicans at the border, who claimed that half of Texas belonged to them. He decided against that. It would be like being in the Army.

He was about twenty miles east of Santa Fe N.M., headed west, when he saw in the distance, one very large tree with smoke from a campfire lazily snaking up through it. His first thought was "hot coffee", he rode slowly toward it. As a safety measure he loosened the extra colt he packed in his waistband for a left-hand draw. His normal dexterity was right-handed, so he packed his holster with another colt low on his right hip. He was almost upon the nine men sitting under the tree before they saw him. Their horses were tied to some bushes nearby. The men all jumped up and went for their guns. No time for reasoning, they were bent on killing him. They did not know Esau, he quickly rolled from his horse and was shooting by the time he touched ground. With two guns blazing, the nine men all died that beautiful evening underneath a century old oak tree. After another century passes, and an interstate highway has by-passed this tree. One can probably stand under it late in the evening when the leaves are not rustling and vaguely hear the nine rapid gun shots. Alike to the proverbial brakeman swinging his lantern on a railroad switch-track in the black of the night.

Esau gathered the dead men's horses and laid each one of them across a horse and tied them to the saddles to keep them from sliding off. He tied each horse together like a caravan and took them into Santa Fe to the U.S. Marshall's office along with a bag full of Yankee currency. The Marshall and his Deputies laid them out on the wooden sidewalk and began the identifications process. Some had papers on them. The others were all known by men in town to be some of "The Wild Bunch" gang.

The Wild Bunch cut a wide swath across Colorado, New Mexico, Arizona, and Wyoming, sometimes reaching into Nebraska, Kansas, Oklahoma, Arkansas and parts of Texas. Two of their known hideouts were "The Hole in The Wall" in Wyoming and the town of Alma in New Mexico.

The Marshall just tagged them as "Wild Bunch" members. He and the Bank of Santa Fe whole heartedly thanked Esau for returning their stolen money. The bank awarded him $1,000. as a reward. U.S. Marshall, Sam Logan issued him a Federal Bank draft in the amount of $4500.—$500. each for bounty on the heads of the Wild Bunch members. Esau deposited the bounty money in a savings account and pocketed the reward money. The infamous leaders of the Wild Bunch, Butch Cassidy and The Sundance Kid, was at that time thought to be vacationing in New York . One famous member who was identified as one of the men Esau Jones killed was Harvey Logan, known as "Kid Curry".

Outlaws have never been uncommon in history, however, there are few criminals that get the recognition of those that lived in America's Old West after the American Civil War. Many of the men who had become accustomed to violence, and often having lost their lands or fortunes, or families, turned quickly to the other side of the law.—and there were those who benefited from the outlaws mistakes. Esau Jones was such a man.

At age 24, Esau was six foot one in his boots, narrow at the hips, wide at the shoulders, handsome with collar length blond hair, brown eyes, and still sported boyish features. He was leaving Santa Fe with almost $1,000, and a sizeable savings account, Esau Jones had found his calling. He now considered himself a full-fledged Bounty Hunter. He outfitted himself accordingly with a new carbine, new boots and a new wide-brim hat. He also bought a bandana, brown in color, folded it into a triangle and tied it around his neck, hanging over one shoulder, so he could pull it up around his face when dust or sand was blowing. He had his big Red-Brown Bay with black mane and tail curried, re-shod and treated to a bucket of oats. The next morning he left Santa Fe with a handful of wanted posters and headed south through Apache territory toward Las Cruces, where he was told he might possible find John Wesley Hardin, an outlaw cattle rustler, bank and train robber that was Texas's most deadly gunman, with a bounty of $5,000 on his head, "dead or alive."

Chapter 1

The frying pan sizzled and smoked as Esau poured cold water into it. He picked up his cup and drank the last of the coffee before collecting his tin plate, coffee pot and frying pan. As he sat on his haunches cleaning them in the small stream, he was taken by surprise at the sensation of a revolver poked into his back. Before his assailant could speak Esau threw the frying pan of water behind him as a prelude to his abrupt turn and attack. As he wrestled his would be assailant to the ground and straddled him—no, it wasn't a him, it was a her, no, not just a her—but a beautiful senorita. He would later find out that in all actuality she was a senora.

"Get off of me, you beast!!" she was hitting at him. He grabbed her wrist and twisted her arms back. "Stop it—stop it now, before I break your arms!" She stopped squirming and tensed-up. "That's better now." he said. "What are you doing out here, fifty miles from nowhere, trying to kill me?"

"I wasn't going to kill you."

"You were making a pretty good attempt at it."

"I was trying to scare you, I only wanted your horse."

"Oh, is that all—well, why didn't you just ask me for'em?" he said sarcastically.

"Would you get off of me?" she asked.

"No!" he glared. "You have to ask nicely."

She stared fixedly into his deep set brown eyes. "Please—?"

Esau turned loose of one wrist, reached over and picked up her pistol.

"Are you telling me that you are out here without a hoss?"

"I had a horse. He was spooked by a rattlesnake and threw me off. He then ran away—probably back to the ranch—would you please get off of me?"

Esau could not but notice that she had on fancy riding britches and hand- made boots. She wore a front-holster with a Double-Bar-M brand sketched in it for her nickel-plated pistol, and sported an expensive sombrero. "*Spanish high-class*", he thought. He noticed too, that she was in her early twenties, and extraordinarily beautiful. He started to unload her pistol, and discovered that it was not loaded. "Where is this ranch you mentioned?—do you live there?"

"Yes, it is my home. It's about eight miles to the southeast, over that saddle-back ridge (she pointed), from atop the ridge you can see the ranch. It's the Double-Bar-M—you're on our property now. In fact, it's a full day's ride in any direction to get off of our property.—I was going to have your horse returned to you when I got home."

"I saw a large herd of white-faced Hereford a few miles northeast. Was them your cattle?"

"Yes, some of them. They say we run about ten thousand head a year."

Esau looked expressionless at her. "That is one hell-of-a-lot of steaks."

"I better get started home—you can get off of me now."

Esau liked sitting astraddle her but he reluctantly got up, extended his hand to pull her up, and handed her the pistol. "Let me pack up my kit and bedroll, and I'll give you a lift home. Why do you pack an empty pistol.—What's your name?"

"Maria—Maria Moynavasa. My husband's name is Enrique Moynavasa. Best if you tread lightly when we arrive, and let me do the talking—the Baron is a very jealous man.—I've never loaded it. I carry it to just make me look tough."

"Then you're a Baroness, what's your full title? It's more dangerous to carry an unloaded pistol than a loaded one."

"Baroness Senora Maria Juana Moynavasa,—yes, I've been told that before."

"Maria, huh—that's a real pretty name."

"Thank you."

Esau, while sitting straddle of her, had looked deep into her beautiful dark lustrous eyes and noticed a slight sensation of innocence.

"You know—I'm really amazed at how fluent your English is."

"I went to school in the eastern U.S."

"You're just plum full of surprises—how long have you been married?"

"Six weeks tomorrow."

Esau looked questioningly into her eyes, "You did say weeks—not years?"

"Yes—six weeks—by the way, what is your name?" She returned his look.

"Esau Jones."

"I've heard that name before."

"Where?"

"I can't recollect when or where—but I know I've heard it. It's a name one doesn't readily forget."

Esau mounted the big Bay and took his left foot out of the stirrup. "Put your foot in the stirrup and swing up behind me. You can sit on my bedroll." They went across the stream and rode toward the ridge.

"It had to be at the ranch, I haven't been anywhere else."

"What?"

"Where I heard your name—It had to be at the ranch."

As they rode up the long slope toward the top of the saddle-back, Maria put her arms around Esau and held tight to keep from sliding back. Her hot firm breast pressed into his back,—burning holes in his mind.—He was ecstatic,—absorbed with erotic ecstasy. *"No Esau, you can't stop, she is a married woman— with a jealous husband."*

Once atop the ridge he could see the ranch on the far side of an extremely wide valley. The large Spanish Hacienda seemed tiny in the distance. Maria loosened her grip on Esau and took her breast out of his back. *"Just in time"* he thought. It was almost a half days ride across the valley at their slow pace. When they arrived there were about forty cowhands readying for a search. Everyone was happy to see her. Her horse had gotten there ahead of her. Baron Enrique Moynavasa helped Maria down from the big Bay and listened intently to her story. Esau dismounted and shook hands with Enrique, a gentlemanly Spanish Land and Beef Baron of about sixty years of age.

"Esau Jones—Yes, your reputation precedes you. You are most welcome, and a special thanks for bringing Maria home safely. You must have dinner with us tonight, and tell me all about the killing of the Wild Bunch."

Maria was flabbergasted at her husband's friendly demeanor. She gave an unknowing shrug to Esau.

"Jose," Baron Moynavasa directed. "Show Senor Jones where to clean up and rest awhile, before dinner."

"Si, Baron" Jose motioned to Esau, "esto modo, Senor". Esau took his saddle bags from the Bay and followed Jose across the courtyard and into a building with many rooms. Jose opened a door and graciously motioned him in. The room was similar to a hotel room. It had a wash basin with fresh water, linens and a bed. Jose with irregular broken English showed Esau how to lock the door from the inside. Esau thanked him with a "Si, Senor" which used up all of Esau's Spanish. He took off his boots and guns and stretched out on the bed. He dozed off dreaming of Maria.—He thought he could still feel her hot firm breast pressing, ever so ravishingly, into his back.

Senor Moynavasa sat at the head of the table with Sonora Maria at the side to his left and Esau across to his right. Seated beside Senora Maria was Senora Rosarita (Rosa) Sanchez, Enrique's sister. Rosa was Maria's Governess during her five years of schooling at Barnard College for Women and Columbia University in the City of New York. Rosa was the wife of Jose who sat next to her. She was herself at one time a very noble and esteemed Baroness before marrying Jose. She also was instrumental in acquiring Maria from a poor village in Mexico when she was but fifteen to cultivate and develop her to the rank of nobility and hold the esteemed title of Baroness, for the express purpose of becoming the wife of Baron Moynavasa.

"Senor Jones, if there is something you wish that is not served, you need but to ask for it. It can be arranged. That was a masterful feat you preformed with the Wild Bunch. I'm sure you tire of talking about it, so I will just congratulate you and leave it at that. There is much of great importance I wish to converse with you relevant to your immediate predicament."

"Ut—oh, here it comes—I guess I was alone with his pretty little Baroness too long."

"Senor Jones, It may come as a surprise to you that I know of your antipathy for the Union Army's redleg militia division. It is known that you have killed many of them. Most importantly to you is the fact that there is a complete regiment of ex-Union Army redlegs assigned to hunt you down, and I know they are closing in. They expect to find you in Las Cruces when you go there looking for John Wesley Hardin.

"How did anyone know I was after Hardin?"

"It probably leaked out from the Marshall's office where you left Kid Curry and the boy's from the Wild Bunch. If you remember, a deputy there told you he could be found in Las Cruces. You will learn Esau, that in this part of the country, which has the reputation of being the bad land— word of mouth news travels faster than if by telegraph.—I have, I guess you would call them, spies throughout New Mexico. They relay news of importance directly to me or Jose.—Now, I'll get back to John Wesley. Before this news broke about you going to Las Cruces to capture or kill him,

"So, being as how my proposition has failed, and I can readily see your point. I suppose you should get a good night's rest before you leave. Let me wish you the best, and if you should ever want to visit or take refuge, I want you to know you are always welcome at the Double-Bar-M. Is there anything you need or we might do for you before you leave?"

"No Sir, not unless you have a Gatling gun." he smiled, "I'll be alright."

"Do you wish a wagon to haul it, or do you want to harness it to your horse? I've seen them harnessed to the front of a saddle at an angle from the withers to the lower chest. Jose can make up a bag of ammunition to equalize the weight on the other side of the horse. That will make it easier on the horse. Just one thing Esau, I would appreciate you not to set up your ambush until you are closer to Las Cruces than you are the Ranch."

Esau was flabbergasted, beyond vocalization.

Early morning after having some breakfast and coffee, Esau went outside and found his horse saddled and ready to go. The Gatling gun and ammunition was securely in place and wrapped with canvas He did not see Enrique or any of the family. He mounted and rode out through the big gate, and turned south which took him into a winding canyon veering to the west. Around the second bend, there she was, in all her radiant beauty, sitting on her pinto horse as if waiting for him. He rode up beside her.

"I wanted to tell you good-bye, and that I'm sorry we didn't get a chance to talk and maybe get to know one another better."

"Yes, I am also sorry. I would have loved to spend more time with you."

"Maybe Esau, there will come a time in the future for us. I will always think of you and wish I was with you."

"Yes, that time may come, Maria."

"I wish it could be now, but Esau I know I'm being watched. So you must ride on and remember I'll always be watching and waiting for you," her voice quivered, "and loving you in my heart." He could see the loving sincerity in her eyes.

Esau prodded his Bay and rode discerningly on down the canyon headed for flat ground, and Las Cruces, with a feeling of blissful despondency, if there be such a feeling.

He wasn't sure, but when he reached the small settlement of San Antonio on the Rio Grande, he figured he was off the Double-Bar-M property. He checked out the sloping ravines from the foothills of the northern San Andres Mountains, which for about a quarter of a mile were almost to the Rio Grande. He could take refuge in one of the deeper ravines and look down and out to the west into the lazy Rio Grande which was about fifty feet across and two to three feet deep. He calculated about two full days to Las Cruces and back, if he hurried. That should put him back about half a day ahead of his arch enemy. He would go take care of business there and double back to meet them here. Esau searched until he found the perfect spot. He unloaded his equipment and set the gun up in some bushes that grew along the edge of a ravine, only about forty feet from where they would pass, or hopefully stop for a swim or to bath in the inviting Rio Grande. The Gatling gun rested on short folding tripod legs near the front and a short folding leg directly in line with the trigger crank, just the right height for shooting from a sitting position. The cartridge hopper was cradled on top of the revolving barrel. It shot .45/70 caliber cartridges, gravity fed into the breech from the hopper. Esau at one time had handled one of these guns before in a battle against Union soldiers when the eighty man Guerrilla troop under the command of William Quantrill rode with General Sterling Price, at the head of 12,000 Confederate cavalrymen conducting a raid on the Union command near St. Louis, Missouri.

Esau did a good job hiding the gun with other limbs of green brush. And he then brushed away his tracks for a good quarter mile, and rode his horse in the edge of the river for about half a mile before getting back onto the trail and pushing the Bay at a fast gait towards Las Cruces. He was somewhat conscience-stricken about even going after John Wesley. Had he not been told that he would be waiting for him, he would have forgotten about it. All for the reason of him being a friend of the Barons. The Baron had told him how much he cared for John Wesley, and how John Wesley helped him out with the cattle. Even for Esau, it is hard to bring himself to kill a friend of a friend.

Perhaps, he thought, it want come to killing. Perhaps he will go to jail peacefully.—Not for a moment did he believe that. Not John Wesley Hardin. Not a gunfighter that has killed over thirty men.

About dusk dark Esau pulled the Bay up near a stream, with a heavy growth of green bushes, that ran into the Rio Grande river. He loosened the cinch on his saddle and left it on the Bay. While the Bay drink his fill of fresh cold water, Esau spread his bedroll out and lay down for the night. He went to sleep thinking about Maria. The more he thought of her, the more he felt that he loved her.

When he awoke at the break of day, Esau put on a little pot of coffee, while he set his mind back on John Wesley. He thought again, only momentarily, about not even going to Las Cruces. But then he must, the man awaits him there. He will check all possibilities of not killing him. He finished two cups of coffee, rinsed out his pot, put it in his utensil kit bag and tied it to a saddle tie. He then rolled up his bedroll and tied it behind his saddle.

After talking to the Bay, and tightening the cinch, he rode on toward Las Cruces. His calculations had him arriving around noon. Maria again began to creep into his mind. Her beautiful smile. Her riding behind him with her breast in his back, and her saying she would always love him in her heart. "Damn'it Esau, stop it." he yelled at himself. "Keep your mind on business. Do you want to get killed?"

After about two hours he had settled down and began to concentrate on his vindictive undertaking back up the river where he left the Gatlin Gun, not giving much thought to meeting John Wesley. He figured that would work itself out when the time came. After all, he's just one man. The abundant number of redlegs will be a complete regiment of at least sixty malicious ungodly scum of the earth.

In another three hours Esau hitched the Bay in front of the saloon with the most horses.

Chapter 2

Last Chance Saloon, Las Cruces, New Mexico. Esau Jones stepped up to the bar and ordered a drink.

"Have you seen anything of John Wesley Hardin, I am supposed to meet him here."

The bartender's glance toward the one busy card table told Esau what he wanted to know.

"Nope, I sure haven't seen him." said the bartender.

Esau downed his drink and strolled over near the card game.

"John Wesley Hardin, you're worth five thousand U.S. dollars to me. I'll collect it alive or dead. I'd rather it be alive out of respect to Baron Enrique, but it's up to you. Alive, you may have a chance in the future, dead it's all over. You've got a couple of second's to let me know which way."

Everyone at the table moved away leaving Hardin staring at Esau.

"Are you Esau Jones?"

"Yes."

Hardin stood up, unbuckled his gun-belt and laid his rig on the table. He put his hands up and moved slowly toward the door.

"The Marshall's office is just up the street." Hardin said.

"Yes, I know. Let's go."

Esau picked up Hardin's rig and they left the saloon. Esau never drew his pistol.

U.S. Marshall, Sam Pickett locked John Wesley Hardin in a cell and put his rig in a desk drawer. "Five thousand, that's a mighty small bounty for ol'John Wesley. You got him right here in town?"

"Yeah, down the street at the saloon."

The Marshall made out a $5,000. U.S. bank draft and had Esau sign his book for it.

"The prisoner wagon will be here in about three weeks, I'll keep him locked up here until it arrives to take prisoners to the state prison near Santa Fe to await trial. Will you be staying in Las Cruces long?"

"Only long enough to deposit this in the bank. I have pressing business back up the river a ways."

"Well, you come back to see me."

"I'll probably do just that."

He went across the street to the bank and decided not to deposit the draft. He instead, cashed it and put the money in his saddle bag. He didn't care to have accounts scattered all across the country, as he figured he would have if he kept on doing it that way. He was expecting to bring in a lot of outlaws, but not all at one place. He got on his dependable Bay and headed out of town the way he had came in. Foremost on his mind was his personal vindication which was about to turn into a full scale redleg massacre. He hoped he was doing the right thing. He knew it could be tricky and most anything could go wrong. But he kept reminding himself about what the redlegs did to his family.

He back-tracked his trail until he came to the southwest end of the San Andres Mountains. From there he followed the western foothills until after dark. He stopped, unsaddled the Bay and rolled out his bedroll. The Bay grazed while Esau slept.

Just after daybreak. He mounted and road on until he found a stream coming out of the mountains. He let the Bay drink while he got out the coffee pot, built a small fire and made coffee. He didn't take time for breakfast but had two cups of coffee before packing his gear, filling the canteen, and heading north at a faster than normal gait. He traveled north most of the day retracing the path he came by. He would occasionally slow the Bay to a slower pace to rest him and then go back to a fast gallop. About two hours before sundown he reached the place where he was to ride in the water, so as to not make tracks, until he got even with the ravine where the Gatling gun was set up. He then led the Bay up the slope to the level spot behind the gun and walked back down to erase the horse tracks. He brushed out his own tracks into the ravine and took his gear off of the Bay, leaving him saddled, and led him further up the ravine behind a shelf area where he could graze. He tucked the Bay's reins under his halter and told him when the shooting started in the morning he was to stay, and keep low. That was nothing new, Esau always talked to the Bay. He had ridden him for a number of years. The Bay had been in many battles with Union soldiers and militiamen. He was wounded three times from musket-balls and twice from bullets. All flesh wounds, that Esau took the slugs from and doctored. He kept the wounds clean and put a salve on them he had gotten from a veterinarian. The big Bay healed quickly. Esau and the Bay were very close friends and understood each other. Esau rolled out his bedroll and laid his carbine beside the Gatlin gun. He figured the enemy to be below him about mid-morning. He was tired, and went to sleep.

When daylight was full blown, Esau was sitting up looking north through an expanding spyglass which he always carried in his saddle bag, along with other usable accessories. Esau got up and poured some cartridges into the hopper from a leather bag which Jose had filled. Esau filled the hopper full and had about enough for two more fill-ups. He picked up his spyglass and looked again. Nothing yet.

The beef jerky Esau chewed on did not go down to well without coffee, but he had water in his canteen. A poor excuse for coffee, but it had to suffice, he could not take a chance on going down to the river and leaving signs. He thought about making it with water from the canteen but it would not be enough. He extended his spyglass and looked again. Still nothing yet. *"My God"* he thought. *"The Bay doesn't have water."* He picked up the canteen and went up the ridge to the Bay. He emptied the canteen into his hat and held it for the Bay to drink. It wasn't much but he was sure the Bay appreciated it nonetheless.

Esau went back to the gun and again looked out toward the northern ridge. There they were coming out of the canyon which he had come out of. He expected them to emerge from further west. They were following his tracks. That meant they came by the Double-Bar-M. That disturbed Esau immensely. He watched them as they veered toward the west and the Rio Grande. He was trying to make out how many there were, and he estimated it to be about thirty. But wait, another troop was coming out further up the foothills. It looked to be about another thirty. *"Why the hell can't they stay together,"* he thought. *"This is going to cause a real problem."* He knew they would reach the river just a little way north of him, and the only logical place to stop and relax in the water is just below him. His only salvation is for the second group to catch up with the first here while the first played and bathed in the water. *"But what if they don't catch up before it's too late."* Esau was in a quandary. A cold sweat broke out on the back of his neck and his brow. The second group wasn't closing the gap.

After watching them come toward him for about three hours, Esau got up and went up to the Bay. He hung the stirrups over the saddle horn. He then took a length of leather from the saddle bag and pulled the Bay down to a kneeling position and had him to roll over onto his side. He tied his front ankles together with the length of leather, rubbed his neck and nose while telling him to lie quite for awhile and be still. *"It won't be for long,"* he told the Bay. He went back to the gun and took his position behind it. He knew he must wait for the second group. As the first group neared him, he told himself. *"Now don't get antsy Esau."*

Just as Esau had suspected, as soon as the redlegs approached the wide area of the river below him, they dismounted and went into the inviting cool water. Some went in fully clothed, others undressed down to their long-johns and hit the water belly first, whooping and hollowing. As they were having a rip-roaring big time, the second group caught up and joined them. Grown men acting like kids looked quite hilarious to Esau. But for him it was vindication time. One redleg was still horseback and slowly riding down the river looking at the ground. It then occurred to Esau that his tracks they had been following were no longer there. Esau picked up his carbine, aimed at the horseman, and one loud lonesome shot rang out and echoed back up in the foothills as the rider toppled from his horse. All of the romping and splashing abruptly ceased and Esau immediately started turning the crank and spraying the water, shooting over the horses, from left to right and back again as Union redleg militia, closer to the far bank, screamed and died. The horses bolted and run down river. Esau lowered his aim to the closer side and continued to shoot back and forth, up and down the river. Some sweeps of the river were dedicated to his Mother, some to his Father and some to his little sister, Susan. *"Like shooting fish in a barrel"* he thought. The Rio Grande ran red that day when about sixty men succumbed to Esau Jones's retribution.

The Bay was happy to get back on his feet, but not so happy that Esau was again loading the Gatlin gun on him. He put the gun slanted from the Bays withers to his upper chest region, as it was when Jose had it loaded. He then led the Bay out of the ravine and up the river about a hundred yards north of the redleg massacre before letting him drink his fill.

Multiple slaughter was nothing new to Esau. He was bred to it in his early years, while riding against Yankee troops and Yankee sympathizers during and after the American Civil War with Quantrill and "Bloody Bill" Anderson's notorious guerrilla bushwhackers. Even so, Esau had a commiserative tender spot. He liked people—who were good and kindhearted.

During this era, killing was bred into literally hundreds of young men, some mere boys. There was no compassion, no sympathy. Killing a man or many men became a way of life brought on by the animosity of the civil war, or as referred to throughout the Confederacy "Lincoln's War." That terminology has rang true for 156 years for Confederate sympathizers throughout the Southland.

An example of the antipathy for Union sympathizers, and the impassioned ease of killing was the Lawrence Massacre led by William Clark Quantrill with the enlisted help of William "Bloody Bill" Anderson, and Archie Clements and their men. The attack on August 21, 1863 targeted Lawrence due to the town's long support of abolition and its reputation as a center for reglegs and jayhawkers.

After a well planned attack the different groups of Missouri riders approached Lawrence from the east in several independent columns, and converged with well timed precision in the final miles before Lawrence, during the pre-dawn hours of the chosen day, all armed with multiple six-shot revolvers.

Between three and four hundred riders descended on Lawrence in a fury. The raiders pillaged and burned the town. They looted the banks and stores, and killed approximately 300 men and boys. The Lawrence massacre was the bloodiest event in the history of Kansas. Esau Jones, the James brothers, and the Younger's took part in that raid.

Was there remorse?—None. Wanton killing had become an excepted way of life for hundreds of Missouri's young men and boys.

Esau rode north almost to the village of San Antonio and turned northeast re-tracing the tracks of the redlegs. He traveled toward the mountainous foothills and the canyon that would lead him to the Double-Bar-M. Dark caught up with him before he reached the canyon. He stopped and made camp, relieving the Bay of his extra burden for the night. He had refilled the canteen at the river, and gave half of it to the Bay in his hat. After rolling out his bedroll it wasn't long until Esau was fast asleep, but morning came early. After a cup of coffee and a piece of hard-tack, it wasn't long until they were again on their way. In a few hours they entered the canyon leading to the Double-Bar-M where half of the redlegs had come out. It was only another hour until they would be there.

Esau saw it before he reached the big gate. The hacienda had been burned to the ground. It still smoldered and smoked. The huge barn remained as did some servant housing. He saw one of Enrique Moynavasa's pistol packing cowhands out near the fence down a way from the big gate covering up a grave. Esau hurried over to him. The man laid the shovel down as Esau dismounted. He had already covered four graves and working on the fifth.

"Who are they." Esau solemnly asked, fearing the answer.

"It's four of the cowhands and the Baron."

"How is the rest of the family?"

"They are safe, they left yesterday."

"Tell me how it happened, did the redleg militia burn the hacienda?"

"Yes Sir, the Baron knew they were coming and he sent Jose, Senora Rosa and Senora Maria away in the carriage and told them to take the route to Santa Fe , by Moriarty and Glorieta so as not to intercept the redlegs, and to go to California. There were only these four hands here, the rest was up north working cattle, a good days ride from here. They say we've lost a lot of cattle up there to rustlers. The Baron made me hide in the safe-room."

"How long were you in the safe-room before you came out?"

"Well, I was there for only a short time before I heard the shooting."

"Tell me about the safe-room, what is it like?"

"It's a camouflaged room with a covered trap door and a basement room. In the safe-room is another one of those Gatlin guns, but they never had a chance to get to it." he motioned to the graves. "It all just happened so fast."

"Have you heard anything from Jose since they left?"

"No, Jose had me to round up two team horses, which we hitched to a two up carriage and they left for Santa Fe about noon yesterday. You know, what I think caused all of this, was right after you left the other day, a friend of the Barons rode in from Santa Fe, and you could tell by his horse that he was riding hard. Anyway, he came to tell the Baron that President Grant, through an act of Congress, had revoked all Spanish Land Grant's. He said that the Barons land was now all open range for everyone to use and build ranches on."

"What is your name?"

"I'm Carl."

"Well Carl, what are you going to do now?"

"I plan on staying here till the other hands get back, and see if any of them would care to stay and make a ranch out of the place and raise cattle. We still have the barn and bunk houses, plus some of the servants might want to stay too. First I've got to make some markers for my friends."

"Carl, I'm going to ride up to the barn. Would you come help me put this gun back in the safe room?"

"Sure, I'll come right now, you would never find the safe room anyway."

Esau had the Gatlin gun off of the Bay by the time Carl walked up. They took it into the barn and went to the far wall. The wall seemed to be the end of the barn. It was impossible to detect that is was set in eight feet from the actual length of the barn. Carl opened a hidden door and Esau took the gun into the room with Carl bringing the cartridge sack.

"There is a trap door under the hay at the end of the room, that goes down to a basement room," said Carl. "But it ain't never used."

"It's an excellent hiding place," Esau said. "Why did the Baron ever have such a place made?"

"I don't know."

"Well Carl, I'm going to give my horse some water and fill my canteen, then I'll be leaving for Santa Fe and see if I can find the rest of the family. You keep those Gatlin guns, you never know when they will come in handy."

"Yes Sir, especially if those redlegs return. I'm going to set one up near the barn door."

"Those particular redlegs won't be coming back, Carl—I killed them—like I said, those Gatlin guns come in handy."

Carl was aghast. All he could say was. "Yes Sir—thank you, Sir."

Esau took care of the Bay, mounted him and headed out—on his way north, remembering what Maria had said to him in the canyon.

The day ended quickly. Esau was near the settlement of Moriarty and made camp for the night. The next morning he found out that the carriage had indeed come through here going toward Santa Fe. He left Moriarty headed due north at a fast gallop and continued the pace most of the day, occasionally slowing down for the Bays sake. A short time before sundown Esau passed the state prison some fifteen miles before riding into Santa Fe. He went to the livery stable and told the man to take good care of his horse, brush and curry him and give him oats and water.

"What's your horse called?" the stableman asked.

"He's called the Bay."

"That's a hell-of-a becoming name." the stableman laughed.

"Have you seen anything of a fine two-up carriage in the last couple of days with three people in it."

"Yeah, it came in early yesterday morning, had three Mexicans in it, a middle-age couple and a younger one, probably their daughter, she was a looker that young one was. The horses are in the corral and the carriage around on the side under the shed. I bought the whole enchilada from'em'" he laughed. "I got it real cheap too."

"Do you know where they went?"

"Yeah, they went to the bank for a while and then they went to the hotel. Later they took the noon stage headed East. Carson, the hotel owner was with them with his horse tied to the back of the stage."

"Okay, thank you, I'll be back in the morning."

At the hotel Esau had no problem finding answers. The owner, William Carson was not of Spanish decent but yet was a close friend of Enrique and Jose. He was the one that rode to the hacienda to tell them about the revocation of the Spanish Land Grants. He was greatly sorrowed when Jose had told him of the impending raid by the Union redlegs. He said that Jose wanted to get Rosa and Maria far away for fear of redlegs coming after them. Jose wanted to take them to Los Angeles. He went with them on the stage to

Tucumcari where they could catch the train to Los Angeles. He told Esau the train came through Tucumcari and veered southwest to El Paso and then west to Lordsburg and on to Tucson, Contention and Yuma where they would be ferried across the Colorado River and board another train to Los Angeles. He then took Esau to the kitchen, fed him and gave him a room for the night.

After much deliberation, Esau decided to ride the Bay to California instead of riding down to Lordsburg to catch the next train which would probably be in another two weeks. William had told him that the train was every two weeks and it was a four or five week trip by horse if he pushed it, and he had no idea where they would be in Los Angeles. He added, "If you find them, let me know that they are okay."

Chapter 3

During the night in the hotel room, Esau had studied his wanted posters and a map to lay out his westward journey. In the morning he went to the bank and withdrew all of the money from his account. He would go get the Bay and head out. As he went out the door he was bumped into by two hombres coming into the bank. There was a seemingly recognizable appearance about them. On the sidewalk Esau pulled the wanted posters from his saddlebag and found them. It was without a doubt, two of Billy the Kid's gang of killers and rustlers. Tom O'Folliard and Charlie Bowdre.

He put his saddlebag back over his shoulder and stepped back into the bank. The two men were at the cage talking to the teller.

"Tom and Charlie. Y'all back up and keep your hands away from your guns."

They did as Esau had directed.

"Now, one at a time, turn and face me. You first Tom and then you Charlie. Now Tom, with two fingers, take your gun and drop it to the floor."

Seeing Esau's look and the gun in his hand, he did as instructed.

"Now you Charlie, the same thing."

Charlie obeyed.

"Bank Teller, will you pick up their guns, I'll get them later."

Esau then marched them out the door and across to the Marshal's Office.

"I have some borders for you Sam."

Esau pulled the wanted posters from his saddle bag and handed them over to the Marshall. The U.S. Marshall, Sam Logan, locked them up and gave Esau a draft for one thousand dollars, five hundred for each man.

"Esau, you ought to get their boss, he's worth a lot more than these two, about ten thousand, last count."

Esau looked at the draft. "Don't have time Sam, I've got business elsewhere. I'll pick up their guns at the bank and drop them by to you."

After going back to the bank and cashing his bank draft. He took the outlaws guns to the Marshall. Again the Marshall told him he ought to get Billy the Kid. Little did he know that at that time Billy the Kid and some more of his gang including Tom Pickett, "Dirty Dave" Rudabaugh and Billy Wilson, were busy driving a heard of Double-Bar-M cattle toward the stockyards at the Wichita railhead.

Esau walked down to the livery stable, paid the stableman, saddled the Bay, and set a bee-line toward Gallup, Flagstaff, Kingman, Barstow and Los Angeles. Four or five hours out of Santa Fe he came upon the Santa Domingo Pueblo where he stopped to water the Bay at the headwaters of the Rio Grande, just a small stream at that point. As the Bay drank, Esau was aware of a man stalking him. A couple of glances told him by the way the man wore his hat and kerchief, that he was one of the men in his wanted posters. Without a doubt it was the Apache Kid, a White Mountain Apache scout and outlaw. Esau was also aware of him edging closer to him. At about a distance of forty feet Esau turned to face him. The Kid, without hesitation, drew on him. Esau shot the gun from his hand shooting off his right thumb in the process. The Kid danced around holding his thumbless hand and making sounds like a scalded dog.

"Why the hell did you draw on me, did you want to die?"

The Kid did not answer. Esau gathered that he probably didn't understand English. He made him wash his wound in the stream and tie his kerchief around it. Esau took a piece of rawhide from his saddlebag and tied it tight around the Kid's wrist to stop the blood flow. With the help of a local Indian, he found the Kid's horse, put him in the saddle and tied his hands to the saddle horn. He led the horse back to Santa Fe, getting there after dark, and went to the Marshals office.

"Sam, I'm glad you're still here. I've got another border for'ya."

"The Apache Kid—hot'damn Esau, you've sure been busy."

"This'un needs a doctor. He accidently lost a thumb."

"Alright, I'll send for ol'Doc Withers." He motioned to one of his listening deputies. The Deputy hurried out the door as the Marshall put the Kid in lock-up.

"Sorry this one ain't worth much Esau." The Marshall said as he made out a draft for two hundred dollars.

"That's alright Sam, hell two hundred is still a lot of money."

"Yeah, I know people that would fill rich with two hundred dollars."

Esau told the Marshall where he captured the Kid, and about the long trip he had ahead of him. The Marshall looked questioningly at him before speaking.

"I don't think you should take that route, Esau. When you get to the high country around Flagstaff and beyond, you're taking a hell-of-a-chance of getting snowed in for the winter. It's too late in the fall to go that way. Your best way would be to go South down the Rio Grande to the pueblo of Hatch and swing west over to Lordsburg. There you could intercept the train from St. Louis to Los Angeles. You could put your Bay in the horse car. It would sure be better than riding horseback all the way to Los Angeles."

"Is that the train that comes through Tucumcari?"

"Yes, that's the one. It's a two week trip from St. Louis to Yuma. It side-tracks there and goes into a rail yard to be turned around and go back to St. Louis. It is turned around there and does it all over again. You'll be put across the river on a large ferry and take another train to Los Angeles. They say the track across the river will be finished in another five years. Southern Pacific has already started putting in the pilings."

"Thanks for the insight Sam, I guess you've changed my mind. I'll be leaving for Lordsburg in the morning. Maybe I'll be seeing you again someday."

"I won't be surprised Esau, you have a way of popping up."

"Oh Esau, by the way, I would travel a few miles west of the Rio Grande on the way to Lordsburg. I hear there are Union Army troops searching the river banks for more ex-redlegs. They've found about forty and you're name is connected to the killing. The redlegs no longer belong to the Army, and the blue-bellies have no reason to, but they probably will arrest you if they see you. So you be careful and don't come in contact with them. Esau thanked him and told him they had about twenty to go. He then took the Bay to the livery stable and went back to the hotel.

William Carson had gotten back from Tucumcari and was surprised to see Esau back so soon. Esau filled him in and told him of his change in plans. Carson also thought the change was best.

"Bill, if they had to wait a few days for the train, I might catch the same run they are on if I hurry."

"Sorry to disappoint you Esau but I saw them on to the train. We only had a few hours wait. It will be in Lordsburg before you get started good.

Esau arose at daylight and had breakfast. He waited for the bank to open and cashed his draft before leaving for Lordsburg. He and the Bay traveled south for two days avoiding the Rio Grande and found their way to the town of Lordsburg. He checked with the train depot and found that he had missed the train by three days. After spotting a troop of blue-bellies on the street he made a quick decision to keep moving. The Bay drank from the trough in front of the depot while Esau filled the canteen and they headed out of town going west.

Dark caught up with them near the town of Bowie in Arizona. Esau made camp just outside of town. He unsaddled the bay and rolled out his bedroll before building a small fire and making some coffee and a cup of corn meal gruel to have with a hard-tack biscuit. He slept while the Bay grazed.

It was easy to spot the hotel restaurant. It was where every horse in town was hitched. Esau hitched the Bay, took his saddle-bag and went inside. The restaurant was crowded and the lady seated him with three cowboys who seemed to be ranch hands. He came to find out they were drifters looking for ranch work. Esau feasted on three fried eggs and steak. Even this far away from the Rio Grande, all the talk was about the ex-redlegs being slaughtered in the river over in New Mexico. That was the first clue to Esau that he was now in Arizona. There were many different opinions thrown around as to the way it happened. The one conclusion culminated by all was that it could not have been accomplished by only one man.

"What do you think?" a man asked of Esau.

"I haven't even heard of it." he lied.

Esau paid the lady at the counter and thanked her for such a fine breakfast. He tied his saddle-bag back on the Bay and headed out toward the west. The day was long and exhausting. He pushed the Bay at a medium fast pace, bypassed Wilcox and slowed down through a rugged boulder strewn canyon known as Texas Canyon, coming out onto a down-slope which lasted almost to the town of Benson. With the sun going down he stopped for the night. He put the Bay in the livery stable to be attended to and got a room at the hotel. After a quick, but pleasant, supper he went to his room. The next day he rode the fifty miles on in to Tucson and did the same thing again, only this time he had a big supper. The next morning he found out that the train for Yuma would be leaving in two days. He bought a ticket for himself and the Bay. On the way back to the hotel he was accosted by four ex-redlegs as he crossed the street. They spread out about forty feet in front of him.

"You're Esau Jones, ain't-cha," said one of them.

"Yeah, and we surely need the ten thousand we can get for killin'ya," another said. "Hope ya'don't mind to much."

"If it's worth dying for? Then have at it. You know I'm going to kill all of you whether you back down or not—so best you go for your pistols now."

They started to draw and Esau let the fastest one clear leather before taking him out with a left hand pistol first and then following suit with both pistols for the other three, two of which never cleared leather. He re-loaded, holstered his pistol, and put the left hand one back in his belt, while waiting for the Sheriff to show up. A number of spectators told the Sheriff that is was definitely self-defense.

"You are free to go, Mister Jones" the Sheriff told him.

"Thank you Sheriff, I'll be catching the next train to Yuma."

"I would really appreciate it if you could lay low in your room until it gets here."

"I'll be glad to do that, Sheriff, except for going into the restaurant to eat."

"Yes, one has to eat."

"Thank you." It seemed strange to Esau that everyone knew who he was.

When the train boarded in Tucson at six a.m. the conductor announced that it would be making rest stops at Red Rock, Contention, Gila Bend and Sentinel before reaching Yuma at six p.m. Esau made sure that the Bay was boarded before he got on the train. He seemed to be in good company with five more fine looking horses. Esau took a seat where he could lean back against his saddle bag and take a nap to the singing rails. It seemed no time at all until the passengers were getting off for a rest break at Red Rock. Esau stayed on the train and took a drink of water from his canteen. He stopped the conductor for a question.

"Sir, were you on this last run to Yuma two weeks ago?"

"Yep, sure was."

"Could you happen to remember three Mexican's, a man and woman, middle aged with a younger senorita with them? They got on in Tucumcari going to Los Angeles."

The conductor looked at Esau and rubbed his chin in an attempt of recollection.

"Yep, by golly I sure do. They were very nice and courtly folks. They transferred on across the river going to Los Angeles, they friends of your'n?"

"Yep, they sure are. Thanks friend." Esau settled back down with a smile of relief on his face. The next time Esau awoke the train had stopped in Contention and the conductor was calling a twenty minute rest break.

"There are sandwiches for sale inside the depot, and don't forget the train will leave at 3:10 for Yuma. There will be two more short rest stops."

Esau decided to get off and buy a sandwich and some strawberry sugar water. That's when he saw William "Curly Bill" Brocious, a known cattle rustler and killer, migrated from the south Texas region to southern Arizona and run with a gang known as the "Cowboys"—all rustlers.

When the train loaded up and left Contention, Esau kept a keen eye on "Curley Bill" to see where he sat. He was in the same car with him but in the other end. Esau secretly watched him until he dozed off to sleep. He seemed to be alone, none of the people around him looked like his type of friends. Esau ambled down to the other end of the car with some leather straps from his saddle bag. "Curly Bill was on his left side fast asleep with his pistol exposed. Esau eased his pistol out of its holster and stuck it under his belt with his other one. He had "Curly Bills" wrists strapped together and tied by the time he woke up, confused and mad. People were looking and wondering.

"Don't be alarmed folks, I am a bounty hunter and I'm taking this man to the Federal Marshall in Yuma. He is a wanted outlaw and killer. Don't be alarmed, I'm taking him to my seat and tying him up better."

All of the people including the conductor watched but said nothing. Esau tied "Curley Bills" feet together and hog-tied his feet to his bound-up wrists. He put him on the inside next to the window. "Curley Bill" was furious but said nothing. Esau did not talk to him.

Esau did not get off of the train at the next two short stops. He gave "Curley Bill" a drink of water from his canteen and offered him half of his sandwich. He refused so Esau enjoyed the whole sandwich and his sugar water alone.

Esau asked the conductor if he knew where the Marshalls office was.

"Yeah, you'll have about a quarter mile from the depot. Most anybody can show'ya."

"When can I get my hoss?"

"Southern Pacific has wranglers to handle the hosses and put them on the train across the river. You don't have to worry yerself about it.'

"How much time will I have to get to the ferry?"

"You'll have plenty of time, everybody takes a break and walks over to the café and eats and then goes out back to the privies, yeah you'll have plenty of time." The conductor turned and made his announcement to the passengers.

"Folks, we are pulling in to Yuma, Those of you going across the river will have a break to go to the café and to the facilities out back before going to the ferry, Thank you." The conductor went to the next car to do the announcement again.

Esau pulled off "Curley Bills" boots, tied them together and hung them over his shoulder before he got him up, put his saddle bags over his own shoulder, got up and led "Curley Bill" barefooted to the exit door awaiting the train to stop. "Curley Bill" looked questioningly at his feet but said nothing.

The Marshall told Esau that he was somewhat expecting him. He said that Sam Logan, the Marshall in Santa Fe was a good friend and he had wired him to watch for you. "He wanted me to let you know that John Wesley Hardin had escaped from the transfer wagon on the way to the prison, killing two guards in the process." Esau showed no emotion to the news. Knowing of Esau's hurry to get to the ferry, he made out the bounty draft for one thousand and directed Esau to the bank where he cashed it and got back to the ferry as it was loading.

On the California side of the Colorado river, Esau first checked to be sure that the Bay was safely loaded into the horse car. He went inside the car, patted and talked to him to let him know he was with him, before boarding a passenger car for the final leg to Los Angeles.

Chapter 4

On the second day after going through El Centro and Santa Ana, the train pulled into Los Angeles. When Esau got off of the train he hurried back to the horse car and watched the wranglers bring the horses down a ramp and hurried over to take control of the Bay. He led him away from the other horses and talked to him while he tightened the saddle cinch and secured his saddle bags. He then got directions to the nearest Federal Marshall's office which was in downtown Los Angeles. He found his way downtown while satisfying his amazement at the commotion and the horse drawn trolley cars. He left the Bay tied to a hitching rail and took his saddle bags with him into the Marshall's office.

"Esau Jones—Yes, we've heard of you. News travels fast among'st law enforcement. With telegraph growing at leaps and bounds like it is, it won't be long before an outlaw won't have a china-man's chance of hiding. My name is Wade, U.S. Marshall Wade Long," he said with a bit of pride in his tone. "What are you doing way out here in California?"

"I'm in search of some friends that disappeared."

"They must have a hell-of-a big bounty for you to travel so far."

"No—no bounty at all."

A gentlemanly looking man, wearing a suit and derby hat, seated by the wall stood up and addressed Esau.

"Could be you would like to work some while you're out here?"

The Marshall interceded. "Esau, this is Eugene Foster, he is a Pinkerton detective. We are looking for the Roy Hobbs gang, a group of outlaws that have notoriously been hitting the banks between here and Monterey. The Pinkerton Agency is the banking administrations security for the west coast and Mister Foster has been sent to work with us in capturing or killing the Hobbs gang."

"Yes, Mister Jones, knowing of your expertise in tracking outlaws, I would be happy to put you on the Pinkerton payroll to help us find these Hobbs boys."

Esau looked inscrutably at Foster and spoke with an impassive attitude.

"Sir, it would be a cold day in hell before I would desecrate my honor by working for the yellow-livered scum that call themselves Pinkerton.—Any low-life sons-a-bitches that would slip up in the middle of the night and throw a bomb into a family home with women and children inside, I hope rots in hell—So you take your job and shove it up your Pinkerton bung-hole." Esau turned and went to the door and turned back.

"Marshall Long, is there any Federal bounty on the Roy Hobbs gang?"

"Nope, not yet Esau, but I expect some will be coming through at any time now."

"Thank you," he said as he went out the door.

Esau searched and asked questions until he wound up in a predominantly Mexican section of town, where he was directed to a Spanish Mission, some two days by horseback, up the coast near Santa Barbara.

He wasted no time in getting to Santa Barbara. The priests name was Ramona Murrieta who took Esau in and talked to him. The first thing Esau did was to ask him if he was related to the famous Joaquin Murrieta. "Not that I know of," he laughed. He listened to Esau's story attentively and with much passion for his plight.

"Esau, are you in love with Maria?"

"I'm opining mightily to that fact. I must talk to her more and get a handle on her resign. I have to find her and then I will know for sure."

"Have you thought about what you will do if you do love her and wish to marry her. You know that bounty hunting is no life for a wife."

"Yes, I've thought about that. If it comes down to marrying I can always get a little farm somewhere. I'm a good farmer."

"Well Esau, your story has touched my heart and I believe you to be honest so I'm going to tell you that there is a new girl in the convent up at the Mission San Miguel Archangel at San Miguel. She is called Sister Maria and is dedicated to being a nun, and yes, there is a Jose and Rosa with her."

Esau was dumbfounded.

"Esau, if you go up there, be sure you are doing the right thing—for her."

Father Ramona Murrieta prayed with Esau Jones for absolution and told him when he got there to ask for the Mother Superior—Mother Angelina."

It had been three long agonizing days from Santa Barbara to San Miguel as Esau dismounted the Bay at the Paso Robles Hot Sulphur Springs Spa about thirty miles short of San Miguel. He figured a good hot sulphur bath would do him a wonder of good before seeing Maria.

Esau walked in the front door which led into a restaurant.

"**AhhhaaaaaOooowaaa**, the spine chilling rebel yell that Esau had not heard for some time, bounced around the walls. It was Jesse James standing with out-stretched arms and Frank seated at the table with a big smile on his face. Jesse and Esau went into a bear hug and danced around the room both talking at the same time. Frank caught them at the table and hugged Esau. "Hey, look at you, It ain't been so awful long ago, you was just a Jackson County towhead." They all sat down. The customers in the restaurant probably had never seen such a joyful reunion among three grown men.

"What in the world are you two doing way out here in California?" asked Esau.

"We could ask the same of you," replied Frank as Jesse sat there with a big smile frozen on his face.

"Our Uncle Woodson owns this spa. Me and Jess come here when we feel like we need to get away for awhile.— Now, what about you, you surely hadn't trailed no outlaws all the way out here."

"Yeah, I heard there were a couple of'em holed up here with big bounties on their head."

Jesse broke out in laughter. "That's right funny, Esau. Now tell us the real reason. This is way too far out of your hunting range. You've become somewhat of a celebrity, you know—a legend in your own time, what with John Wesley and the Wild Bunch."

Esau told them about Maria and the Baron. He told them the whole story right up to being just half a day from her, and being scared to death to go see her. Frank and Jesse were unaccustomedly humbled and felt sorry for their cold hearted bushwhacker friend.

"I think all of the cabins are taken," Frank said. "But we can get another bed and put you in with us. Uncle Woodson is out of town right now but he'll be back tomorrow. You need to stay for a few days and get yourself relaxed. We'll go down to the bath houses this evening and soak in the yellow water."

"Yeah," Jesse said. "You'll like that—it'll make you feel lots better. You can tell us about all the redlegs you've killed while we soak. It seems that you've about eliminated them."

"Not hardly Jess, but I've made a big dent in their numbers."

"Where is your hoss?"

"He's at a hitching rail out front."

"We have a couple in the back corral. We can put him in with them. We only bought them yesterday. We came out on the train but decided to buy the hosses to go up in the gold country and see if we can find where our Paw is buried." They were walking out the front door as Jesse talked.

"Hey, you've still got the Bay." Jesse rubbed the Bay and told him hello. They then walked the Bay around to the corral behind the cabins. Esau took off the saddle and bridle and the Bay checked out the other two horses. As they came back around the cabins Frank and a hired man were bringing a single bed to their cabin.

Further down from the cabins were six or eight bath houses. Some of them had a single tub and others had two or three tubs. One house had six tubs in it. "It's for community baths," Frank mused. The white porcelain bathtubs with naturally hot sulphur spring water piped to them were stained to a golden honey color from the sulphur. Each bath house also had a clear water shower in it.

After three days of visiting and soaking in the hot sulphur water, Frank and Jesse headed out for Angels Camp on the Stanislaus river in Calaveras County after telling Esau to let them know of his outcome. Esau, feeling much better, headed to the Mission San Miguel Archangel some thirty miles to the north.

Esau was amazed at the size of the mission with numerous buildings built of red clay stucco and showing years of degradation. He found a hitching rail in front of the biggest building. As he removed his saddle bags and put them over his shoulder he saw about six nuns in work clothes and their habit head covering planting seed in a garden. A lady without the head covering seemed to be instructing them. As he approached them he noticed that the lady was Senora Rosa. She looked up and saw him.

"Senor Jones, you did come, Maria said you would." She seemed delighted to see him. She showed the young nuns what to do and took Esau to a round stone table with chairs around it and graciously asked him to have a seat.

"Senor Jones, I am exceedingly pleased to see you. We heard, even before leaving Santa Fe, about the ranch burning at the hands of the redleg militia. We only learned of the saddening demise of Baron Enrique after arriving in Santa Barbara. Senor Carson of the Santa Fe hotel, whom had taken us to the train, sent a telegram to Father Morrieta in Santa Barbara whom in turn related the atrocity to us when we arrived there. Senor Carson also said the bounty-hunter had eliminated the redleg militia. We assumed that he must have meant you. That is why I am so happy to see you. Taking on feats like that is living dangerously and one wonders if they will ever see you again."

"Senora Rosa, God rides with me everywhere I go." Under the circumstances Esau thought it proper to leave the impression that he was a God fearing man. "Your brother was given a proper burial, near the front entrance, at the ranch. Where is Senor Jose?"

"I believe he's back at the stable grooming Mother Angelina's carriage horses."

"And how is Maria?"

"She is now Sister Maria and she is doing well. She is living at the convent and has dedicated her life to God. She is to be a teacher of children. Mother Angelina is expecting you. I'll take you to her."

Esau followed Rosa into the building through huge double doors and down a hall to the Mother Superiors office. Rosa tapped on the door before partially opening it and announcing Esau's arrival. She stepped back and motioned him in. The Mother Superior stood up behind her huge desk and directed him to sit down. Esau took his saddle bags from his shoulder and laid them, along with his hat, on the floor beside the chair before sitting down.

"Esau"—the Mother Superior said as she studied him. "I've been looking forward to meeting you. Your parents, I'm sure are fine God loving people to bestow upon you such an exquisite and masterful name."

"Thank you Mam, yes, they were, but I lost them near or after the end of the war."

"I'm so sorry—tell me Esau, about your life and how you lost your parents."

Esau told her the whole sordid ordeal of his young life riding with Quantrill and Anderson and about the Union redleg militia burning the home and killing his parents and little sister and how he came about turning to bounty hunting and how he met Maria and was overtaken with love. He added that it was not lust but truly a caring and meaningful love and he came to California to find out if she felt the same as he, as she had once indicated. And that he found out only after arriving that she had become a nun and was living in a convent.

The Mother Superior was a most complacent and friendly woman in her mid-sixties. Esau's initial fears were unfounded and he felt at ease with her almost immediately.

"I was expecting a Priest. It surprised me that there wasn't one."

"No, I've been running the mission and convent for over twenty years. My name is Sister Angelina Louise, but I'm always referred to as Mother Superior. Jose Sanchez, Rosa's husband, is the only man living here. Senor Jose brought me a book from town a few days ago. It's what is called a dime novel and it's about you. The title is Esau Jones, The Outlaws Nightmare, and subtitled The Demise of the Wild Bunch. Have you seen it?"

"No Mam, I haven't heard nothing about it."

She handed him the book and he thumbed through the ten or twelve pages with hand drawn action picture inserts. The front cover, in blazing color, was a hand drawn picture of a man standing straight up with two guns blazing and men falling. Esau laughed.

"I've seen books like this of Jesse James and other outlaws, and one of Wyatt Earp, but I don't know why they would make one of me. They sell them in newspaper stands and mercantile stores. I haven't been in such a place in some time. None of the books are depicted as the events really happened."

"I'm sure they glorify the stories to sell books."

"Yes Mam."

"It will soon be dinner time. You can leave your saddle bags and hat, and your guns, in back of my desk here and I'll show you where to wash up and then I'll take you to see Sister Maria for a little while before we eat. Now, I'm sure you understand that Maria has dedicated her life to God, and your presence is going to cause a mental stress on her, so don't be demanding. She will have to work this out in her own time—with a lot of prayer."

Esau was not in the least uneasy about leaving his belongings in this room but he did however feel somewhat naked without his guns. He followed Mother Angelina through the building to a room where he washed his face and hands. She was down the hall talking to a couple of sisters when he came out and she took him further down the hall and tapped on a door before opening it.

"Sister Maria, there is someone to see you. Sister Leona, you can come with me. Sister Maria, bring the gentleman to the dining room with you when the bell sounds." Maria's roommate, Sister Leona came out the door and stole a quick glance at Esau as he went in. The Mother Superior pulled the door closed. Maria stared at him as if in shock. They were both completely immobilized until Maria grabbed him and hugged him like she was never going to let him go. She finally did, but only to kiss him repeatedly.

"Esau, I have longed for you every day, even that first day on your horse when I held your strong body next to mine.—I knew I loved you even then, and I knew you loved me too. It's just one of those things a person feels—have you felt it too Esau?—did you know you loved me from that first day?"

"Yeah, Maria—I felt it and I do love you. What are you doing in a convent?"

"Jose and Rosa brought me here. They said we would be safe here and they and the Mother Superior talked me into joining the convent. It sounded like the thing to do, I always listen to Rosa and Jose, they being my Godparents. I have refrained as yet from taking my vows, but I have dedicated myself to the work of God, and am being schooled in the teaching of children."

They heard the bonging of the large bell as Jose struck it repeatedly with a large wooden hammer. Maria, with her face flushed from the kissing, put on her habit headdress and went out the door firmly holding Esau's hand. She turned loose of his hand as they entered the large dining room. About twenty nuns seated at the huge table were stealing quick glances at Esau as Maria and he sat down. Mother Angelina stood up and announced that the visitor was a friend of Maria's. With no further explanation she said grace over the food and everyone ate without talking.

The outcome of a meeting between the Mother Superior, Maria, Esau, Jose and Rosa was culminated with the Mother Superior's decree that Maria shall stay at the convent until Mister Jones can show the responsibility of housing her with a job unrelated to killing. If he truly loves her as he professes, he will work toward this end, while Maria continues her schooling," she said.

Rosa followed Esau to his horse and told him their contact would be William Carson of the Santa Fe hotel and to take care of himself.

Esau Jones rode away from the mission suffering an excruciating mental torment such as he had never before known. But he knew now, as the sweetness of her warm moist lips lingered in his mind, that without a doubt he did truly love Maria, and he also knew she loved him. His mind was in a quandary as to the predicament that the Mother Superior had leveled on him. In the final conclusion of his agonizing situation he reckoned the only thing to do was try to bring in as many wanted outlaws as feasibly possible. It was a matter of making enough money to support Maria, as the Mother Superior had said.

Instead of stopping at the Paso Robles hot sulfur springs, Esau stopped in town at the hotel. He did not wish to burden Mister James with his problems, knowing he would ask about the outcome of his plight. He had been such a generous and kind man, like all of the James clan that he had known as a boy.

He put the Bay in the livery stable and passed on supper. Probably the only time in his life he didn't feel like eating, he went directly to his room. To deviate from his anguish, he put his mind to work on planning his action of bringing in outlaws. Where to start? Where would he find the most action? New Mexico? Arizona? Texas? The accumulation of his jumbled thoughts were only adding to his distress, so he went to the restaurant and drink three cups of hot coffee. He decided to get the next train back to New Mexico, and return to Santa Fe. As good a starting place as any, he figured he could debark at Santa Rosa, which would be closer than Tucumcari, to ride back to Santa Fe.

Upon asking a local man about the train service from Paso Robles to the ferry at Yuma, he discovered that a train went south every three days, straight through San Diego and over to the Yuma crossing, where then it was every two weeks going east to Saint Louis and connecting to Chicago and New York. It was more than Esau needed to know but he graciously thanked the gentleman and went up to his room where he further pondered his decision to go to Santa Fe. Was he making the right move? Were there any outlaws left there? Should he maybe get off in Las Cruces? His mind raced a mile a minute and fell into a state of semi-befuddlement.

Chapter 5

Mid-morning after having a sleepless night in the Paso Robles hotel some forty miles south of San Miguel, Esau had a small breakfast and retrieved the Bay from the livery stable. He started to head to the train station when he was witness to the town bank being robbed. The bandits were hell bent for leather after running to the side of the bank where the eighth man held the horses. Esau took note as to the getaway route they took going west and into the rugged mountainous region. He followed their trail cautiously at a slower pace than they were going. It was easy for Esau to follow their fresh tracks higher and higher into the mountains through arroyos and canyons. About mid-afternoon he came upon a wooded glen. He could see a small frame cabin through the trees with the bandits horses tied in front of it. Hiding the Bay behind a thick growth of saplings he slipped through the woods to within fifty feet of the cabin and stepped into the opening in front of the cabin.

"Hello, the cabin!" yelled Esau. It only took one yell and four men came scurrying onto the porch.

"What do you want—who are you?"

"I want to see Roy Hobbs about a job!"

A fifth man came onto the porch. "How did you get here, come inside where we can talk."

Esau figured this one to be Roy. "Are you Roy Hobbs?" he asked.

"Yes, I'm Roy, come on inside the cabin."

Once inside the cabin one of the men anxiously declared, "Roy, this is the man in my book. He is that Jones man. The one that killed the Wild Bunch!"

"Hobbs, I'm not here looking for trouble. I've a proposition to make you."

"You're the one in that book, are'ya?"

"Yes, I'm Esau Jones. I've collected more bounties than probably anyone."

"That's what you want?—to collect a bounty on us?"

"Like I said—I've got a proposition. I hope you know, I could kill all of you very easily if I was so a'mind—and today I'm really in a killing mood. You know the vile low-life Pinkerton's have a ten thousand dollar bounty on you and your gang. So instead of collecting the bounty, I'm going to let you pay me the ten thousand to stay alive. And you should better tell this man by the wall to my left that if his hand gets any closer to his pistol that you and he will die first."

"Aubrey, hold your hands up, damn you man, hold them up!—Why are you in a killing mood today, Mister Jones?—it ain't because you don't like the Pinkerton's is it?"

"No Roy, it's because I'm madly in love with a nun."

"Aubrey, get that bag out of the nail keg and give Mister Jones ten thousand dollars. That's not much for our lives boys, so be happy."

Esau walked Roy back to the Bay, thanked him, and rode away with ten thousand dollars in his shirt. After back-tracking his trail and coming out near dark at the same place he had started from, he put the Bay in the livery stable and got a room at the same hotel just as dinner was being served. Feeling a little better he ate supper, and went to his room, and counted his bounty savings. Including the ten thousand from Hobbs he had twenty-one thousand and seven-hundred dollars. He was still living off the one thousand reward money given him by the bankers in Santa Fe for returning the stolen money from the Wild Bunch and he still had plenty left. Esau went to sleep wondering what size farm he might could buy and still have money left to live on until he got the farm going. He tried to keep his mind off of Maria so he could sleep, but it didn't work to well, her beautiful smile kept interrupting. He pondered her thoughts about living on a farm. Maybe she would like ranch life better or perhaps raising hosses. "Yes, that's it." he declared aloud. "We could raise fine riding hosses, the best quality like bays, roans, chestnuts and buckskins. I wouldn't want them on open range like in New Mexico. In Missouri we could have the ranch fenced in. Yes, I'm going to look into starting a hoss ranch back home in Missouri. I think she would like that. It would beat dirt farming all to hell."

Early next morning Esau bought passage for him and the Bay to Santa Rosa, New Mexico. Santa Rosa as yet was not a regular train stop for lack of a Depot and services, but they would stop and put Esau and the Bay off. The clicking of the rails helped him to get some sleep as they traveled through Los Angeles on the way to Yuma, ferried the river, went through El Paso and up to Santa Rosa where he and the Bay got off and he rode back west to Santa Fe so he could talk to Carson at the hotel since he was to be the contact between him and Maria. Also he knew with plans for a ranch he was going to have to make a passel more money.

At the hotel in Santa Fe, after leaving the Bay at the livery, he cleaned his guns and talked to Bill Carson. Bill had not yet heard from Jose but said he looked forward to it. "They are good people and will do what they say. I'm happy that you and Marie are somewhat betrothed."

"Have you heard from Carl or any of the ranch-hands?"

"Carl was here, he left just yesterday to return to the old ranch. A handful of the ranchers stayed on with him to try to build it up, but they're having a hell'of'a time trying to make a go of it, what with the range wars going on. They managed to sell off some of the Double-Bar-M cattle. That's what they're living on right now. Most of the herds have been rustled."

"Bill, I'm going to take the stage to Tucumcari and wait on the next train to Kansas City. From there I'll ride my hoss down to Independence. That's the closest big town to my old home. I'm going to look for some property near there to buy, so you can reach me by mail at the post office there,—now that's Esau Jones, post office, Independence, Missouri. I'll check frequently for any word from you. And next time you see him, give Carl my address."

With the Bay tied to the back of the stage, Esau and a group of other people set out for Tucumcari. Only about three hours from Santa Fe, and thirty minutes past the Pecos stop, two outlaws, Buck Barrow and Leonard Cox attempted to rob the stagecoach. They had the shotgun guard to throw down his shotgun and the strongbox and ordered the passengers to get out of the stage. As one of them dismounted his horse to collect the passengers valuables, the shotgun guard in an attempt to stop them pulled his sidearm. When the mounted outlaw turned and shot the guard gave Esau the split second he needed to gun them both down. The guard was only wounded in the shoulder. Esau and the driver tied the men over their horses and Esau on the Bay took them back to Santa Fe. The stage returned to Pecos to have the guards wound attended, before going on to Tucumcari.

Marshall Sam Logan and two deputies saw Esau ride up with them.

"Esau Jones, you know, I kind'a figured it was about time for you to bring me in somebody. Thought you were in California. Take them off the hosses boys and see who we have here. What happened in California. Did you find your people?"

"Hey boss, this here is Buck Barrow and Leo Cox."

"Yeah Sam, I found'em."

"Where is your girl, I'd like to meet her."

"She's still in California, she'll be coming later."

Sam felt the tension in Esau's voice like he didn't want to talk about it so he dropped it. "Let's see what these two are worth and you can tell me how you got them. While Sam looked through some posters Esau explained to him about the stagecoach robbery attempt.

"There's five thousand on each one of them. I'll make out the draft for'ya and then let's go have some supper."

"I'll be right back, I need to take care of the Bay."

"Okay,—you're on for supper?"

"Sure."

As usual Esau had his saddlebags slung over his left shoulder as he and Marshall Logan went into the hotel restaurant and sat at a table. Bill Carson saw them and went over to their table.

"Hi, Sam—Esau, I thought you left on the stage?"

"Yeah Bill, but I got side-tracked. The stage was held up just past Pecos and I had to come back."

"Yeah Bill." Sam said. "He brought back the robbers, Buck Barrow and Leo Cox."

"You got'em locked up, Sam?"

"Naugh, my boys took'em over to the undertaker."

"Oh,—you needing a room Esau?"

"Yeah."

"I'll leave the key on the desk. It'll be for your regular room."

"Okay Bill, thank you."

Esau opened up and told Sam of his plans of raising the best in riding horses and settling down in Missouri. He told him of his love for Maria—and that she was now a nun, but later they would be married.

"Holy shit, Esau, I never heard of anybody marrying a nun. Man, if you ain't always full of surprises. Holy shit, you're really gona marry a nun."

He told him that he would have to work awhile first. He told him where he could be reached in Missouri and said he would stay in touch. They finished eating in silence and Esau went up to his room.

The next morning Esau decided to just ride the Bay to Tucumcari. He cashed the ten thousand dollar draft and put it in his saddle bag with the other bringing his total up to thirty-one thousand, seven-hundred dollars.

After riding back through Pecos and heading east through mountainous passes he stopped high in the mountains and made camp for the night. He made coffee at daybreak and warmed by his campfire. It was quite cold as he rolled up his bedroll, warmed his hands again and drank his third cup of coffee. He did not make any breakfast because he figured he had been eating too much.

He rode down through the eastern slopes of the mountains and through the foothills coming upon a stream as he entered flat ground. The Bay was happy for the water as was Esau. According to Esau's map he should be only about ten or fifteen miles from Las Vegas where he would have flat ground east bearing a bit south to Tucumcari. As Esau started to mount the Bay he noticed a man breaking camp about fifty yards down stream. The man had his back to him, saddling his horse, and did not see him as he gingerly approached from the opposite side of the stream. When Esau was within about fifty feet of the man he was almost assuredly that it was Billy the Kid by the crazy hat he wore which he had seen on his poster.

"Hello, Billy," he said loudly as he drew his right pistol and pointed it at him. Billy turned quickly reaching for one of his pistols and just as quickly held his hands out away from them. He grinned sheepishly.

"Hey man, you'd just sneak right up unbeknowest on a feller, wouldn't you."

"Take them two little ol'pistoles out of your belt, one at a time, with two fingers, and drop them on the ground. Any funny move and I will shoot you right through your heart.

The Kid, still grinning, did as Esau said. Esau then, with a leather strap tied the Kid's hands firmly behind him. After making the Kid sit down and remove his old bedraggled boots, he pulled the Kid's horse's reins over the horses head and let them drop to the ground, before helping the Kid onto the horse and strapping his feet together under the horse's belly. He then tied the end of the reins together, mounted the Bay and led Billy the Kid, singing, toward Las Vegas.

In about three hours they were at the Sheriff's office in Las Vegas where the Kid was put in manacles and leg irons and locked up. The Sheriff knew nothing of any federal bounty but said that New Mexico's governor, Lew Wallace had placed a five hundred dollar bounty on him. The Sheriff went to the telegraph office with Esau and wired the Governor about the capture by Esau Jones. The Governor in turn wired the Las Vegas bank to pay Esau Jones his promised bounty. It took a couple of days but Esau collected his bounty and headed for a three day trip to Tucumcari.

In the interim Henry McCarty, aka Henry Antrim, aka William H. Bonney, aka Billy the Kid was transferred to Santa Fe, where he wrote to Governor Wallace seeking clemency. Wallace, however, refused to intervene, and the Kid's trial was held in Mesilla. After two days of testimony, McCarty was found guilty of the murder of Sheriff William J. Brady. Henry McCarty was sentenced by Judge Warren Bristol to hang. With his execution scheduled for May 13, Billy the Kid was removed to Lincoln, where he was held under guard by two of Sheriff Pat Garrett's deputies, James Bell and Robert Ollinger, on the top floor of the town courthouse. While Sheriff Garrett was out of town, Billy the Kid stunned the territory by killing both of his guards and escaping.

It is believed that a sympathizer placed a pistol in a nearby privy that Billy was permitted to use, under escort, each day. Billy retrieved the pistol and turned it on Bell when the pair had reached the top of a flight of stairs in the courthouse. Bell fell and rolled down the stairs, gut-shot he staggered out into the street and collapsed, mortally wounded. Billy worked his wrists out of the manacles and scooped up Ollinger's 10-gauge double barrel shotgun and waited at the upstairs window for Ollinger, who had been across the street with some other prisoners, to come to Bell's aid. As Ollinger came running into view, Billy leveled the shotgun at him, called out "Hello Bob" and killed him.

The Kid's escape was delayed for an hour while he worked free of his leg irons with a pickaxe and then he mounted a horse and rode out of town singing.

Lincoln County Sheriff Pat Garrett whom had been after McCarty since the end of the Lincoln County War responded to rumors that McCarty (then going by the name William Bonney) was lurking in the vicinity of Fort Sumner. Garrett and two deputies set out to question one of the town's residents, Pedro Maxwell, whose sister Paulita was a girlfriend of Billy's. Pedro told them "yes" he thought Billy was in town.

It was contended that Garrett went to the bedroom of Pedro's sister Paulita, and bound and gagged her in her bed. When McCarty or Bonney arrived, Garrett was waiting behind Paulita's bed and shot the Kid dead.

McCarty was buried the next day in Fort Sumner's old military cemetery, between Tom O'Folliard and Charlie Bowdre. A single tombstone was later erected over the graves, giving the three outlaws names (Billy as "William H. Bonney') and with a one word epitaph of "Pals" also carved into it.

Like many gunfighters of the "Old West", Billy the Kid enjoyed a reputation built partly on exaggerated accounts of his exploits. McCarty was credited with the killing of 15 to 26 men, depending on which biography one reads.

A number of the deputized Regulators with whom he rode to keep the peace between two competing factions faded away or secured amnesty, but McCarty was in no position to accomplish either. His negotiations with governor Lew Wallace (famed Union Civil War General and author of the novel *Ben-hur: A Tale of the Christ*) for amnesty came to nothing. His position was further undermined by a string of negative newspaper editorials that referred to him as "Billy the Kid". When a reporter reminded Wallace that the Kid was depending on Wallace's intervention, the governor supposedly smiled and said, "Yes, but I can't see how a fellow like him can expect any clemency from me."

One widely reported characteristic of McCarty has stood the test of research: his personal charisma and popularity. Various accounts recorded by friends and acquaintances describe him as fun-loving and jolly, articulate in both his writing and his speech, and loyal to those for whom he cared. He was fluent in Spanish, popular with Latina girls, an accomplished dancer, and thus especially well-loved within the territory's Hispanic community. There he was regarded as a champion of the oppressed. "His many Hispanic friends did not view him as a ruthless killer but rather as a defender of the people who was forced to kill in self-defense. In the time that the Kid roamed the land he chided Hispanic villagers who were fearful of standing up to the big ranchers who stole their land, water, and way of life.

Chapter 6

Esau had long since gotten off the train in Kansas City, Missouri and rode down to Independence, where he deposited $42,000. in the bank in both his and Maria's name. He had spent the last three months looking over his homeland, remembering his childhood and finding the markers he had left for his family. The old home place was about halfway between Lone Jack and Pleasant Hill. This area had all been sacked and burned by the redleg militia. Blue Springs, about forty miles south of Independence had also taken its share of desecration but some buildings were left and many people had or were rebuilding. This area between Blue Springs and Lone Jack, about thirty miles north of the old farm, is where Esau had decided on trying to find a place for his horse breeding business. He remembered that the Younger's had been raised only about another twenty or thirty miles to the east and that Jesse and Frank's home, in Clay County, was about forty miles north of Independence.

After finding the old farm, the first thing Esau did was to have his Mother, Father and little Sister's remains exhumed, put in caskets and placed in the Blue Springs cemetery.

During the Civil War, Jackson County was the scene of several engagements, the most notable of which was the battle of Westport, sometimes referred to as the "Gettysburg of Missouri." The decisive Union victory here firmly established Northern control of Missouri, and led to the failure of Confederate General Sterling Price's Missouri expedition, although battles fought in Independence, Blue Springs and Lone Jack resulted in Confederate victories. Jackson County was heavily affected by Union General Thomas Ewing's infamous General order No.11. With large numbers of Confederate sympathizers living within its boundaries, and active Confederate operations in the area a frequent occurrence, the Union command was determined to deprive Confederate bushwhackers of local support. Ewing's decree practically emptied the rural portions of the County, and adjacent Counties. From Kansas City, one could see the dense columns of smoke arising in every direction, symbolic of a ruthless military despotism which spared neither age, sex, character, nor condition. The legacy of Ewing's imbecilic order would haunt Jackson County for decades to come.

Only about three miles out of Blue Springs going east toward Lone Jack on a tree shaded road, Esau had stopped more than once to admire the large plantation home sitting back near some one hundred yards from the road. He had been told that it had been spared the desecration of other places because Union General Thomas Ewing had commandeered it for his campaign headquarters during his surge through southwest Missouri and southeast Kansas.

Esau would sit on the Bay looking at the mansion with its six huge white columns rising two stories. He would admire the beautiful grounds and daydream about having his horse ranch here. He would talk to Maria about it and give it to her for a wedding present before coming to his senses and back to reality. He knew that there was no way he could ever afford to buy it, so why torment himself, and he would ride on looking over the countryside. He found a forty acre plot near Pleasant Hill that looked good and had a stream running through it. A house would have to be built, and barn, stable, and holding corrals for in-heat brood mares. He sure didn't want to mix breeds. The sign said to see the Blue Springs Bank. He wanted more than forty acres but he thought he would inquire anyway, but first he would go to Independence and see if he had any mail. Disheartened that there wasn't any mail for him at the post-office, and knowing that he would need more money, Esau went to the U.S. Marshall's office in Kansas City, introduced himself, and ask to see the wanted posters. The Marshall, Henry Hancock, introduced himself, sat Esau at a table and brought out a stack of posters about a foot high.

"Out of these you can keep the ones that interest you, Mister Jones, it seems that every ex-guerrilla fighter turned outlaw after the war."

"Yeah, I know, it's a shame isn't it."

"I guess they had to do it."

"Yeah, I guess so."

"Oh, here's a new poster on the "Willy Bunch." He reached into his desk and handed it to Esau. "They are four men that work together—bank robbers." Henry was reading the poster. "There's Jim and Otis Willy, Earl Hickok." He looked at Esau. "Probably no relation to Wild Bill.—Then there's Rufus Musgrove—Hey, in fact it is said to be them that robbed the Jefferson City Bank a couple of days ago,"

He looked back at the poster. "They're a long way from their stomping grounds. They usually work Ohio and Indiana." Henry handed the poster to Esau.

Esau took the poster and laid it to the side as he went through the stack of posters one at a time and occasionally laid one to the side. Most of them were ex-Quantrill guerrillas, men who Esau knew well and would not bring himself to hunting. The eleven posters he kept were of Richard "Big Dick" Ingram, Pliney Gardner, John Kinney, Henry "Snake Eyes" Smith, Bill Miner, John "Bigfoot" Matson, Tom "Blackjack" Ketchum, Shirley Reed "Belle" Starr, Thomas Daly, Billy Milner and Jessie Evans.

Esau studied the Jessie Evans poster. He believed he knew his whereabouts. It had to be the nervous young man that sat across from him on the train from Tucumcari to Kansas City. He also got off in Kansas City. He had no horse with him and the last Esau saw of him was when he got off and went toward uptown, packing a luggage bag with some ice rope tied around it to keep it from coming open. Esau's curiosity was jarred by a round silver pin on his lapel with the letter "B" engraved on it. It was the same kind of pin worn by Billy the Kid when he was subdued. So he inquired from the conductor as to his boarding. He had gotten on the train in El Paso.

The Jessie Evans gang, also known as The Boys, was a gang of rustlers and robbers led by outlaw and gunman Jessie Evans. The gang was formed after Jessie Evans broke away from the John Kinney gang. After breaking away he brought Billy Morton, Frank Baker, Tom Hill, Dolly Graham, George Davis, Jim McDaniels, Buffalo Bill Spawn, Bob Martin, Manuel "Indian" Segovia and Nicholas Provencio into The Boys.

The gang initiated numerous acts of robbery and cattle rustling, mostly committed in New Mexico. Evans and other gang members killed Pancho Cruz, Romabin Mes and Tomas Cuerele at the Shedd's ranch at San Augustin, Dona Ana County, and then shifted their domain to Lincoln County, New Mexico. They raided John Chisum's ranch, whom Evans had once worked for, and the Mescalero Apache reservation. They continually rustled cattle by the hundreds from the southern sections of Baron Enrique Moynavasa's vast Double-Bar-M ranch. It is believed that at this time Billy the Kid rode with them.

At the outside of the Lincoln County War the gang was hired by the "Murphy-Dolan faction", to harass the Latter's opposition in Lincoln County. They began by rustling the cattle and horses of the "Tunstall-McSween faction." A posse was dispatched by Sheriff William J. Brady to arrest rancher John Tunstall. The posse included Jessie Evans, William Morton, Frank Baker, Tom Hill and Dolly Graham, all members of Jessie Evans' gang. They ambushed and murdered Tunstall which ignited the Lincoln County War. Several days later, the Lincoln County Regulators, a vigilante posse formed by Tunstall and McSween supporters and at that time led by Dick Brewer caught Morton and Baker, and executed both men. On that same day Jessie Evans was injured and Tom Hill was killed while attempting to raid a ranch near Tularosa. Evans was arrested but managed to break out of jail. Evans returned to Lincoln and was present at the five day siege at McSween's house, known as the Battle of Lincoln.

After the war he and Billy Mathews are said to have attempted to make peace with Billy the Kid, but the two killed lawyer Huston Chapman, putting them on the run from law enforcement. The gang fled down to Texas, but Texas Rangers began pursuing them relentlessly, and killed several gang members including Dolly Graham. The Rangers caught up with the gang, including Jessie Evans, in Presidio del Norte, Mexico. The gunfight that followed would mark the end of the Jessie Evans Gang. The Rangers engaged them in a shootout, during which Jessie Evans shot and killed Ranger George Bingham, and Ranger D.T. Carson was wounded by other gang members. In turn, Ranger Carson and Ranger Ed Sicker shot and killed gang member George Davis, and shot and wounded gang member John Gross. The remaining members were captured. Gross was sentenced to a long prison term, but spent less than four years. Jessie Evans was sentenced to ten years, but while on work release he escaped, and disappeared.

"Marshall, could you direct me to a livery stable with a hotel close by?"

"The hotel is directly across the street and the livery stable is at the end of the street to your right."

"And where would the disreputable section of town be?"

"One block straight over," he answered with an inquisitive tone.

Esau thanked him and left.

Call it intuition or ??, Esau was sure that high-strung man was Jessie Evans, so he set out to find him. He would go to the section of town where such a man could easily loose himself. The dark slums of back street flop houses, saloons, whore houses, and gambling halls.

Esau took the Bay to the livery and this time he left his saddle bags with the saddle. As he walked back down the rather busy street to the hotel to register he was acutely aware of people watching him. The restaurant looked inviting so after registering he had coffee, three eggs, ham and biscuits with red-eye gravy. He then returned up the street to the barber shop to get a clean shave. In all actuality he was killing time until late evening when the disreputable back street would be in full swing. When the soothing hot towel was removed and the barber began to lather his face, the first thing Esau saw was the burnt-red leather leggings standing just inside the doorway. The man slowly walked over in front of the barber chair.

"Esau Jones—It seems, I caught your ass off guard, don't it. I been living for just this day."

"Then I guess your living must be all done."

The redleg pulled his army colt and a shot rang out loud and long in the little room as the sheet covering Esau flew into the air and across the room from the combustion of Esau's colt. The redleg was hurled against the wall and slid down to the floor dead from a shot through his heart. The sheet fluttered lazily down the wall, covering the dead redleg. Esau had the barber to finish shaving him as he told the Marshall what had happened. The barber collaborated Esau's story of self-defense.

The Marshall had some men take the dead redleg to the undertaker. Esau offered to pay the barber for the sheet with the hole in it. The barber refused and said he would display it on the wall for people to see while he told them the story. Esau signed his name by the hole at the request of the barber. He then decided to go to the hotel and lie down for a while.

When Esau started to go up the stairs he noticed a bag in the darkened corner along by the side of the stairs, it was the bag tied with ice rope. The hotel manager told him, "The man what owns it was a guest for nigh on to two months, he left the bag when he checked out a few days ago and said he would be back for it. He ain't got back yet. He could'of kept his room, ya'know, but he didn't want to spend the money."

"What name did he register under?"

"Tom Hill's his name, he's a right nice feller too."

"Did he say where he was going?"

"Nope—but I know though."

"Where?"

"He was going over to Fort Osage to collect some money the Army owed him for some horses he sold'em a while back that were shipped from New Mexico. He should be getting' back by now, he's on a horse that belongs to the livery. You know we own the livery too."

As Esau turned to go upstairs the front door opened.

"Hi Sam, I'm back, you about to give me up?"

As the man walked toward the desk, Esau approached him with his left hand gun being pulled. "Hello, Jessie."

Evans froze and paled as Esau took his gun.

"That's not Jesse," the manager said. "I know Jesse, that's Tom Hill."

"Sorry, Sam—this is Jessie Evans, and we're going to stroll across the street to the Marshall's office."

Esau was issued a ten thousand dollar Federal bank draft for the bounty on Jessie Evans. He spent the night at the hotel, ate a hearty breakfast and returned to Independence where he deposited the draft into his and Maria's account bringing the total up to $52,000. He then checked the post office and had no mail so he went on down to Blue Springs and inquired at the bank about the forty acre plot down near

Pleasant Hill. The bank owned the property and said they would have to have eight thousand for it and added that it had a small stream running through the middle of it with two natural springs. Esau thanked him and said he would ponder it. It wasn't the price. It was the mere fact that he didn't think it would be big enough. At least he got an idea what land was going for and would start looking more. He knew he needed enough land so the horses could run and kick up their hoofs.

Esau left Blue Springs with the intention of riding east on over around Pittsville and look around some more. A few miles out of Blue Springs he came to that beautiful plantation home again. He had to stop and fantasize living there with Maria.—Or just living anywhere with her—God, how he so wished she was with him. Esau knew she was better off right now where she was, and he knew he had to stop his brooding, least it affected his wits and reflexes in a scrap. So, Esau decided then and there, that he would put his mind on bringing in more outlaws. Good breeding stock cost a lot of money. He went back to the Blue Springs hotel, got a room, and studied his wanted posters until about supper time. He took off his right-hand rig and left it and his hat in his room.

The turnip greens and corn-pone was exceptionally good. "This restaurant sure does a good business," said the gentlemen seated at the table with him.

"Do you live here in Blue Springs?" asked Esau.

"Nope, just passing through. Me and my three partners, back at the corner table are on our way to Topeka. That's in Kansas, ya'know. Do you farm around here?"

"Yeah, something like that.—How long does it take to ride from Jefferson City?" he took a bite of turnip greens followed by a big bite of corn pone as the man readily answered him.

"It takes nigh on ta'three days."

"Sure been nice weather, ain't it." Esau got up and sauntered into the lobby and then rushed up the stairs to his room, put on his right gun-belt, got his hat and went back down and out the front door, circumventing the restaurant and out to the hitching rails. There they were, four very fine, and hard rode horses. Esau quickly went to each horse and loosened the saddle cinches. Then he sat in a chair in front of the hotel and waited.

In a short while the men came out of the restaurant and attempted to mount their horses and went crashing to the ground as their saddles slid underneath their horses bellies. The frightened horses backed out into the street, raring up and bucking.

Esau stood on the walk in front of the dumbfounded men. Esau got their undivided attention by firing a shot into the air.

"Jim Willy, I'm taking you boys to jail. Unbuckle your rigs and drop them to the ground. If you want to die, reach for your gun."

Rufus Musgrove did. Esau let him clear leather before shooting him through the heart. The other three hastily dropped their rigs to the ground and held their hands high. Esau directed them to the Sheriff's office where the three men were put in shackles and held for the U.S. Marshall in Kansas City who in turn, with many telegraph wires, had them moved by Deputy Marshall's, back to Jefferson City to stand trial. The Jefferson City Bank had all of its money returned. It had been divvied up and was in the four outlaws saddlebags. In the aftermath, the three outlaws were found guilty and received light sentences due to the fact that they had not killed anyone and the bank got its money back. However, they would be extradited to Indiana and then to Ohio to be tried for numerous bank robberies.

Esau rode back up to Independence to check with the Post Office and deposit the money from the draft on the Willy gang. Five thousand each for the Willy gang dead or alive brought Esau and Maria's account at the Independence Bank up to $72,000. Esau had contemplated moving their account to Blue Springs. He had initially picked the Independence Bank because of its location in a bigger city and it's less vulnerability to robbery than the smaller bank in Blue Springs, not being aware that customer deposits were insured by the banks protection agency as were train robberies, which at this time was the nationwide Pinkerton Agency. It would be some time in the future before FDIC would come into being. Esau, knowing nothing of how the banking industry worked decided to leave their account in Independence. Also he was unaware that one of Frank and Jesse's Uncle's was the President of the Blue Springs Bank making it off limits for robbery, in respect and admiration of Frank and Jesse.

Honor among thieves, or be it what it may. Outlaws, Bounty hunters, Yankee killers or Preachers of kin. There was an unwritten law that kept them united . Esau would not hunt the multitude of outlaws that rode as bushwhackers, and no outlaw would dare rob a James banker.

Had Esau known that the Pinkerton Agency was underwriting customer protection insurance, as it was the loss of shipments from train robberies, there would be no telling what his reaction would be. Probably something like what happened in Los Angeles at the Marshal's office with the Pinkerton detective, Eugene Foster, who tried to hire him to work for him.

Esau harbored a severe hatred for the very name "Pinkerton", almost with the same bitterness as he held for the damnable redlegs.

Chapter 7

After leaving Independence with still no mail it occurred to Esau that they were probably waiting to hear from him. He had decided to go back to Blue Springs to have supper and visit with the Sheriff. He had failed to even get his name. He had been very gracious about holding the Willy's and Earl Hickok, and taking care of the dead one. Then he figured he would get a room at the hotel and compose a letter to Bill Carson in Santa Fe and ask if he had heard from either Jose or Rosa Sanchez, and inquire as to the well being of his beloved nun, Maria.

The first thing Esau did was to stop at the Sheriff's office. The Sheriff was elated to see him. After a few pleasantries, they exchanged names. The Sheriff's was Mathew Murdock. He knew Esau's, said he had read four paperback novels about him.

"I hope you didn't believe everything you read."

"Naw, some of it seemed a little far-fetched." They both laughed.

The talk soon got around to Esau's plight and plans. Esau told him how much he admired the big plantation home outside of town and about Maria and the plans for trying to find a place to settle down and raise horses. The

Sheriff filled him in on the history of the plantation. After General Ewing left the house, his troops had orders to spare the house and property because he was led to believe that the Bumgartner's, owners of the place, was dyed in the wool Union sympathizers, when in all reality they were whole heartedly behind the rebel cause. The Bumgartner's had moved to Blue Springs fifteen years earlier from near Baton Rouge, Louisiana because of the areas predominate Protestant religious denominations. Fredrick Bumgartner had the home built to his wife's specifications. It sat on 360 acres of beautiful rolling hills with small stands of hardwood scattered throughout and a meandering creek running across the back section that was fed by numerous natural springs. The Bumgartner's raised fine bred horses for the prominent horse lover.

"Then about a year ago Fredrick's wife died of tuberculosis, and he just gave up. He only has a couple of buggy horses left on the place and is trying to find a buyer for it. He don't want to live there without her.—If I was you Esau, I'd talk to him when he returns. Maybe something could be worked out. There are a few people left out there that worked for him. They are hanging on to see what happens. They live in those houses down the line to the left of the big house, and I believe there are some servants and a cook still in the house. They are colored people, slaves who did not want to leave when set free."

Esau was utterly captivated by the Sheriff's story. "Do you think there is a chance I might could buy that place?—Return from where, where is he?"

"He went to England. He will return in the Spring. There is a caretaker out there too if you would like to look the property over, I'll go with you, he want mind at all."

"Three hundred and sixty acres—good gravy!—yeah, I'd love to see it."

"How about in the morning after breakfast?"

"Sounds good, Matt, I'll be here," with a big smile, he shook the Sheriff's hand, and headed for the livery stable and then the hotel. Esau slept very little that night. His mind raced a mile a minute on expectations of looking over the property and writing to Bill Carson with something positive to tell Maria and her God-parents. The only problem is, he doesn't have any positive news yet as to settling down. He decided to wait on writing to Carson.—*"God, I wish I could see Maria and hold her close to me and tell her I love her."* He instead had decided to go to Kearney, up in Clay County, to see Mrs. Samuel, Frank and Jesse's mother, to find out where he might find Frank. He needed to ask him if he knew the whereabouts of Rufus Henry Ingram. He himself vaguely remembered Rufus riding for a short time with Quantrill's Raiders. He didn't stay long and it was whispered that he was a Yankee spy. The poster he has on Rufus has this history and a fifteen thousand bounty on him dead or alive to be paid by the chicken-shit Pinkerton Agency. *"What the hell,"* Esau thought, *"I need all I can get right now."*

In 1863, Rufus Henry Ingram met George Baker from San Jose, California, who had just come east to join the Confederate Army. Baker complained because the secessionists in California had no experienced leaders. Ingram claimed to have been with Quantrill Raiders during the Lawrence Massacre (a bald-face lie, Esau thought) and became interested in going back with Baker to recruit soldiers for the Southern cause.

In early 1864, Rufus Henry Ingram arrived in Santa Clara County with a Confederate commission as Captain and with a former undersheriff of Monterey County, Tom Poole, organized about fifty local Knights of the Golden Circle and commanded them in what became known as Captain Ingram's Partisan Rangers. Finding difficulty in raising funds to purchase supplies for his unit, Ingram first planned a raid on San Jose to rob its banks and stores in the manner of Quantrill's raid on Lawrence. A quarrel within the band, however, led to the exposure of the plan to the local Sheriff and it was abandoned.

Soon after, Ingram decided to rob shipments of silver from the Comstock Lode to Sacramento. Ingram, along with a small detachment, robbed two stagecoaches eleven miles east of Placerville of their gold and silver, leaving a letter explaining they were not bandits but carrying out a military operation to raise funds for the Confederacy. During the pursuit of his fleeing band, the posse had a gunfight with two lawmen at the Somerset House. One of the posse was killed, while Poole was wounded and left to be captured. After a two day chase the Placerville posse lost their trail and they managed to get to Santa Clara County a week later. Tom Poole gave a complete confession, the bullion was recovered and he exposed his companion's identities. Regardless, they evaded the search for them in Santa Clara County.

An attempt by Ingram to rob the New Almaden Quicksilver Mine payroll failed, ending in a shootout with the posse of Santa Clara County Sheriff John Hicks Adams a mile and a half outside San Jose on the Almaden road. Two of Ingram's men were killed, while one of his men was wounded. The Sheriff and his Deputy were also wounded in the shootout. Ingram fled California for Missouri and was never captured.

When Esau and the Sheriff went out to the plantation, the first thing he saw going up to the house was three huge live oak trees off to the right of the front yard with a beautiful white gazebo nestled in the middle of them.. He met the caretaker, Jim Conners, and walked around to the back where he was elated to see a stable with six first class stalls, holding pens and a training corral. In the corral he saw two beautiful, leopard-spotted, Appaloosa geldings. Jim told him they were trained for carriage horses, and were the only two horses left on the farm except for some personal horses of farm hands still living on the place.

While domesticated horses with leopard spotting patterns have been depicted in art as far back as Ancient Greece, the Nez Perce people of the United States Pacific Northwest developed the original American breed.

Esau would anxiously await the return of Fredrick Bumgartner, and see as the Sheriff put it, if something could be worked out. He then took a jaunt up to Kearney, in Clay County, and about four miles to the farm of Reuben Samuel and Zerelda James Samuel, mother of Frank and Jesse. Zerelda knew him right away, although she had not seen him since he was a boy.

"Esau, Glory be my boy, (she held out her arms, the right one off below the elbow), it's so good to see you."

"Yes Mam, you too," he bent down and kissed her on the cheek. "It has been a long time."

"Yes, Lord how Mercy, I was taller than you, now you done gone and passed me way up."

"Yes Mam, I didn't mean to. I'm a'looking for Frank, thought you might could tell me where he's at."

"I spoze I could, Esau, he's a'standing right over younder in that doorway."

Esau looked around and saw Frank leaning against the door-facing of a bedroom, smiling at him."

"Hey Frank, if you'd be a rattlesnake, I'd done be bit. I must be losing it." They both laughed and went into a bear hug. "I thought I'd have to trace you down, but here you are at my first stop."

"He slipped in unbeknowest to me," Zerelda said. "And was down in the kitchen poking around in the coals to heat up the coffee pot. Like to have scared the living daylights out'ta me."

"Can't a man come ta'see his mama?"

"Yeah sure, I always figgered you for a mama's boy." He stepped behind Zerelda and held her by her shoulders, as if shielding himself from Frank.

"Well, tis true Frank," Zerelda said. "You always was."

"Now y'all gon'na gang up on me. What did ya'want to see me about Esau?"

Esau turned loose of Zerelda and kissed her cheek again. He sat down on the settee and looked seriously at Frank.

"I wanted to get your opinion on Rufus Henry Ingram. Was he really one of us, or not?—and where might I find him."

Frank pulled up a straight chair and sat close to Esau.

"Rufus, huh—you're dredging up old memories best left forgotten."

"Was he a Yankee spy?"

"I really don't think so, but the whole family was certainly Union sympathizers. He wasn't with us long enough to really get a good fix on'em."

"Wasn't he with us at Lawrence?"

"He went there with us, but it was a decisive opinion that he left shortly after the campaign started.—Why the interest in ol' Rufus?"

"The interest is fifteen thousand dollars bounty for robbery and murder in California. I needed to know if he was one of us."

"No, I think it's safe to say he was not one of us.— Did ya'find what you were looking for after you left Uncle Woodson's place?"

"Yeah, what about you and Jesse, did you find what you were looking for?"

"Naw.—Did you bring the lady back with you?"

"Naw,—She had joined a convent—but I'll bring her home as soon as I get a home to bring her to."

"Joined a convent, huh."

"Yeah, seems I'm in love with a nun."

"Lord help'ya, Esau boy." Zerelda said. "Would it be ya'just don't understand the ways of life? I'll pray mightily ta'God for'ya, boy."

"In love with a nun." Frank shook his head compassionately.

"Do you know the most logical place he might be, or where his family was located."

"Best I can recollect Esau, was his folks lived somewhere north of the Chillicothe in a cabin located on a river. I never knew the name of the river and I'm not real familiar with the country up there." I remember the talk was that his paw was a trapper."

"Thanks Frank, I'll do some checking on it."

"In love with a nun huh,—Esau boy—you ain't sick, are'ya?"

"Naugh, I feel just fine, Frank."

Heading northeast for two days without seeing anything resembling a river, Esau abruptly came upon it. A bridge made from heavy timbers over a rushing river. A sign burned into a flat surface on the end of the bridge read, "Grande River bridge built by Union Soldiers." Esau crossed the bridge and camped for the night. The next morning after coffee he continued up the road and in less than an hour he was in Chillicothe. He went into a Lumber Camp commissary and inquired as to a trapper named Ingram. The man in charge said he didn't rightly know that name. An elderly man playing checkers overheard the conversation and spoke up.

"His name's Henry, Henry Ingram. He was in here just a couple weeks back. Had a wagon loaded down with his stuff. Had another man helping him and had a Indian squaw too. Had a lot'ta stuff, he did. Said he was a'moving down stream to where it emptied into the Locust. The Locust is a bigger river, it is. He figured it to have more Beaver on it."

"How far is it downstream to the Locust?"

"Probably about thirty, maybe forty miles," said the man in charge.

Esau bought some peppermint stick candy and a couple of apples for the Bay. The apples were beginning to wither so he cut one open and checked it for juice. It was better than he had imagined so he bought two more. Outside, he took the bit from the Bays mouth and gave him the cut apple. He put three in the saddle bag, then they went back to the river and headed southeast, following the river downstream. About an hour before dark Esau made camp. He had a piece of dried beef with a hardtack biscuit and a cup of river water. When morning came he made himself some coffee and gave the Bay another apple.

By mid-morning he had reached the Locust river and since he was on the down side he followed it for a little way. Spotting a hill some distant away from the river, he went to it and rode up the grade a way, before stopping and dismounting. He took his extending spyglass from the saddle bag and began to study the river from where he had left it to a few miles further down. It was probably about three miles further down the river where he spotted the wagon in a stand of cottonwood trees. He also thought he could make out a couple of lean-tos under the trees and some pelts hanging between two trees. He put the spy-glass back into the saddle bag and led the bay back down the hill. When he reached the river he mounted the Bay and rode on down the river, as best he could tell, about two miles. He then hobbled the Bay in some tall grass, gave him the last apple, and sucking on a piece of peppermint candy, he started moving quietly down the river.

It wasn't long before he heard a distinctive chopping sound above the sound of the rushing water barreling over some boulders. He moved cautiously toward the chopping sound and saw a man cutting down about a foot wide tree. He felled the tree and began to trim it clean of its limbs. He discerned that this had to be Rufus and not his Dad Henry. He took note that he was not wearing a sidearm and that his horse was tied nearby. Esau was almost upon him before Rufus detected him. Rufus started to make a dash for his horse where there was a carbine in the rifle scabbard. He stopped dead still when he saw Esau draw on him. Esau circumvented him and went to his horse. He took the carbine and slung it into the river. He searched the saddlebags for pistols and found none. He then made Rufus sit down on the ground.

"Rufus, take off your boots."

"Why?"

"Because I said so, and I'm the one with the gun."

Rufus pulled off his boots and Esau picked them up one at a time and threw them in the river. "Good Lord, Rufus, your feet are rotting. I never smelled nothing so terrible in all my life as them boots. You better be glad I throwed'em away."

"Am I spoze to thank'ya?"

"That's just up ta'you, you'll probably be cussing me time you walk barefooted for a spell."

Esau untied Rufus's horse and led him as they walked back to where the Bay was. He then took some leather straps from his saddle bags, made Rufus get on his horse and tied his feet into the stirrups. He then tied his hands behind his back, tied the end of the reins together, got on the Bay and led Rufus's horse back up the Locust river. By dark they had reached the Grande River where they camped for the night. After taking Rufus off his horse, he untied his hands, got a bar of lye soap from his own saddlebag and told Rufus to sit down by the river and wash his feet. Esau shared his covering with Rufus and made coffee enough for both in the morning. He then headed back the way he had first came, and camped out three more nights before reaching Kansas City where he went directly to Marshall Henry Hancock's office.

Esau left Rufus tied on his horse and went into the Marshall's office. "Hey, Henry, I've got Rufus Engram outside for'ya. Have a couple of your men to untie him and lock'em up. If'n you will get him a plate of food from the restaurant, I'll pay for it. He ain't ate nothing for three days."

Two deputies brought Rufus through the office headed for the cells. Marshall Hancock looked at him as he passed. "Esau," he asked. "Where are his boots"

"He ain't got none," Esau answered. The Marshall let it go. The next morning after the Federal business proceedings were transacted, Esau went down to Independence and deposited the Federal bank draft for fifteen thousand to his and Maria's account bringing the total up to $87,000.

Esau did wonder occasionally about Rufus's Dad and his Squaw. *"But hell,"* he thought, *"he made out without Rufus most all his life anyway."* Esau was a congenial type of man. He was like-minded and pleasingly sociable with his fellow man. In all reality he detested killing people and did so only when necessary, excluding redlegs and the killing during wartime. He figured that didn't count, it was a necessary obligation to the Confederacy. He truly did think sympathetically about Rufus's Dad, and wished well for him. He knew he was a good man with a hard, but honorable profession in the selling of Beaver pelts.

Even though he hated killing, it came as a way of life that he was bred into at an impressionable age, and it came easy. He could still remember the first four men he killed after joining the Quantrill raiders. They were a unit of only about forty members, but growing daily. They raided a group of Yankee cavalrymen while they bivouacked for supper. As they rode up on them from two sides, the soldiers ran for their horses and Esau dropped four of them before they could mount. The other raiders got the rest of them. Esau had no qualms or remorse. In fact he remembered having a good feeling when he shot the damned blue-bellies.

And so, it was like that throughout the war and after, during reconstruction.

Since he has been a Bounty Hunter, his mind-set has increasingly changed to a sense of detest to have to kill a man, but unfortunately it does occasionally have to be done.

Chapter 8

Esau rode down past Blue Springs and sit on the Bay looking at the plantation home while daydreaming about Maria. This, and the Blue Springs Lake, seemed to be the only place that he could release his inhibitions and think clearly. He had fleeting thoughts about going back to California to see her. Not being able to see her or knowing how she was gnawed at him constantly. He sat there on the Bay and made up his mind. He was at least going to Santa Fe and find out if Bill Carson had heard anything and possibly going ahead and writing to her.

On his way back to Kansas City he stopped at the Bank in Independence and drew out $1,000. He and the Bay took the next train through Tucumcari on down southwest to Vaughn, which was one days ride west, to the burned out Double-Bar-M ranch. From the barn, Carl saw him ride through the front gate, and went out to meet him. He and eight other cow-hands were still trying to hang on and salvage what was left of the stock.

"We have about forty head of Hereford up close to Moriarty. The boys have gone to drive them down here close to the barn. Rustling is still a major problem and we need to get all of them we can in close so as to keep an eye on them."

"How far is Moriarty from here?" asked Esau.

"It's not far, just a short day's distance."

"Isn't that on the way to Santa Fe?"

"Yeah, it's another two days on to Santa Fe."

Esau told Carl about going to California and finding Maria, Jose and Rosa. He told him about being in love with Maria, and about him trying to find a place in Missouri to raise top grade horses. And make a home for the three of them, and about quitting bounty hunting.

"Esau, you know I'm tickled to death, but how are you gon'na get her away from that convent?"

Esau stared blankly at him.

"You know I been talking to Carson. He told me all about it, he just didn't tell me your side of it—ain't many people ever married a nun."

"Well, this one is gon'na."

"Well, Easu, you know I wish the very best for both of you."

"Thanks."

"Listen, when you get the horse business started, I may be asking you for a job. I know lots about horses, especially good full breed ones."

"Sure Carl, you can always find me through the Independence Bank. That's about twenty miles south of Kansas City—I'm going on up to Santa Fe. I'll look in on the hands near Moriarty if I see them."

"Okay thanks, I always worry about them out on this damn open range."

Esau made camp about twenty miles shy of Moriarty. The next morning he was up and gone before sunup. He reached Moriarty without incident, no cowboys and no cows. He saw a crowd in front of the Sheriff's office.

"Hey Esau," a cow-hand approached him as he got off of the Bay. "My name is Ed Trusdale, I'm from the Double-Bar- M. Rustlers hit us at daybreak this morning. It turned into a gun battle and two of our men were shot. They are in the Doctor's office right now. Our other four men are over there with them. Last we saw the rustlers were driving the cattle east, toward Santa Rosa. They appeared to be some of the remnants of the Billy the Kid gang."

"How bad off are the two that got shot?"

"The doctor said that they would pull through, he had to remove a bullet from each of them."

"Has the Sheriff or a posse given pursuit?"

"Naugh, the Sheriff here ain't gon'na do nothing."

"Listen Ed, You leave one man here to see to the two injured ones. Tell him, when they can ride, to go back to the ranch. Then bring the others and go with me, we will catch up to them tonight, they can't drive cattle at night."

"What are we gon'na do?"

"We're gon'na get the cattle back and then y'all can take them to the ranch."

"Alright Esau, if'n you say so."

"How many rustlers are there?"

"Bout five best I could tell."

"That all, you go take care of things at the Doctors office, then y'all meat me on the trail east."

Esau tarried until the four men caught up to him. He made introductions all around and sized them up. One of them looked like a born gunslinger. The other three, including Ed, seemed somewhat nervous. They only traveled about twenty five miles, it was getting dark, and the rustlers had bedded the cattle down for the night. Esau and the boys kept a distance and made a quiet and fireless camp. They discussed how they were going to do this without stampeding the cattle. Esau said to leave it up to him. He told them to get some sleep.

In the wee hours of the morning Esau got up, untied the Bay, and slipped out of camp. After leading the Bay for a ways, he mounted him and rode quietly toward the rustler's camp. He tied the Bay to a bush and slipped into their camp with his leather straps. He was glad to see that they were not sleeping close together. One after the other, he cracked them across the side of the head with his pistol barrel, before rolling them over and tying their wrist behind their backs. While they were knocked out, he took each of their gun rigs and their boots off, tossing them into a pile. As they came to their senses he helped them one at a time, get on their horse barefooted and tied their feet into the stirrups. He took a lasso rope from the saddle tie of one of the horses and threaded it into a saddle ring on each horse securing it on the last horse and then tied each of the horse's reins to the rope leaving about a four feet distance between each horse. He got the Bay and led the grumbling and cursing outlaws like a caravan toward the other encampment. It was daybreak and the boys were up wondering where Esau was when he rode up leading his caravan of rustlers.

"Boys, ya'll can get your cattle and take them home. Tell Carl I'm gone to Santa Fe.—By the way, there are a pile of boots and pistol's where they were camped if y'all can use'em. A couple pair of boots had damn nice looking Mexican spurs on'em."

"Why didn't you get yourself a pair of em?" Ed asked. "You're wearing them little'ol rounded-off soft spurs."

"If'n you train your hoss right you don't have'ta cut up his hide with sharp spurs. My hoss does what I ask of him with these little'ol soft spurs."

The following day around noon, Esau and his caravan of outlaws rode up the street to the U.S. Marshall's office. Sam Logan was on the walk in front of his office grinning from ear to ear.

"What'cha got there Esau."

"Just a few cattle rustlers Sam. You want to take them off my hands, I'm tired of'em."

Sam called his Deputies out of the office. "Alright boys, y'all was looking for something to do. See about locking these five men up and start identifying them."

"I was told that they were some of Billy the Kid's gang, if that will help," said Esau.

"I think you're right," a Deputy said. "I recognize two of'em."

"Sam, if you can take it from here, I need to go over to the hotel and get a bath and talk to Bill Carson."

"Yeah, we've got it Esau."

Esau first took the Bay down to the livery stable and then came back across the street to the hotel. As was the norm he had his saddlebag over his shoulder when he saw Bill Carson and told him he had been up for two nights, and needed a tub of hot water in his room to take a bath, and he would talk to him after getting a nap. Carson had a Chinaman to take care of getting the bath ready, gave Esau the key and told him to give the man his clothes for washing. "It's good to see you Esau, yes we have a lot to talk about," said Carson.

85

Esau, after taking his bath and going to bed, did not awaken until sometime in the night, too late to talk to anyone, so he went back to sleep. After daylight he found his clothes outside his door, cleaned and ironed, he got dressed and went down the stairs. Bill Carson was in the lobby and he asked Esau if he was ready for some breakfast. They went into the restaurant and sat at a table.

First things first, Bill told him that he, just a couple of days ago, got a letter from Jose. He took it from his shirt pocket and gave it to Esau.

The letter was short and to the point. *Hello, my amigo, I hope this finds you well, Maria watches for the mail daily, hoping to hear from Senor Jones. Rosa and I can tell by her eyes that she cries every night. We worry immensely about her well-being. If you can in any way get a message to Senor Jones. Tell him to please write to her.—My deepest regards, Jose.*

Even though slight, Carson could see the moisture in Esau's eyes.

"Bill, is it possible to send a telegraph wire to the mission?"

"I don't see why not,—the only draw-back would be getting the telegraph office to deliver it."

"Let's try it. Let me have your pencil."

Esau turned the letter over and wrote on the back of it. *Mission San Miguel Archangel—San Miguel, California— Sister Maria Moynavasa, My darling Maria, sorry I've been so long in writing. I've been very busy in looking for the most fitting place for my angel to live. I've decided that we will legitimately raise and sell the very best in riding horses. Hope this meets with your approval. I'm in search of our home and property in Missouri where I was raised.*

I choose Missouri because there is no open range, I can fence our land. I will either find or build us a suitable home. Give my best to Jose and Rosa, and to Mother Angelina. With all my love, forever.—Esau

Esau handed the letter to Bill.

"Let's have coffee and breakfast and then go to the telegraph office—Tell the dispatcher to wire some money along with it for the delivery man to take it to the mission."

"Wow, that's the longest wire I've ever seen, it's gon'na cost you a fortune to send."

Esau did not comment. He was busy ordering breakfast.

At the telegraph office the dispatcher ask Esau if he wanted him to cut it down some for him.

"No, I want every word put in it just as it is written, and I want some money sent for delivery."

"How far is it from the telegraph office in San Miguel?"

"It 's about five miles from town. I guess that's where the telegraph is."

"Then I'd say we send about five dollars."

"Send twenty, I want to be sure they deliver it."

Bill Carson was hanging back taking it all in as Esau did it himself. Esau was feeling better about himself now that he was, in a sense, contacting Maria.

The dispatcher got through, counted the words and added the twenty for delivery and told Esau his tab was seventy-two dollars. Esau handed him a hundred dollar bill and told him the change was for him for doing a good job.

Esau and Bill went to the Marshall's office to check on the identifications of the rustlers.

"Hey Esau, hey Bill, how are y'all on this beautiful morning." He picked up a piece of paper. "Esau, we got'em all I,d'ed. They are sure'nuff remnants from Billy the Kid's defunct gang." He read the names from the paper. "Jim French, John Middleton, Fred Waite, Henry Brown and Frank Coe." He pushed his open book over toward Esau. "Here, sign my book for your money." Esau signed the book as Sam handed him the draft for $2,500.—five hundred for each man.

Bill went with Esau to the bank. He praised Esau for what he had done and wished the best for him and Maria. Esau cashed the draft and put the money in his saddlebag. They went back to the hotel restaurant for some more coffee.

As they drank coffee and discussed Esau's proposed venture into the horse business, Sam Logan came in and joined them. He listened intently to Esau's depiction of breeding within the true lines of different breeds, including the lines of brood mares in order to keep the bloodline pure.

"What breed do you intend on raising?" asked Sam.

"Not only one breed, but various breeds like for instant Roan's, Sorrel's, Buckskin's, Palomino's, Paint's, Bay's,— by the way, I have a great full blooded Bay stud down in the livery stable to start with,—he will service only full blooded Bay mares," he laughed. "That is the only way to keep the bloodline pure and produce the very best in riding horses and working ranch horses. However, with a good full bred stud it is possible to get fine stock with interbreeding a mixed brood mare. I won't only be breeding them, the farm will also break and train them."

"He has it all worked out Sam—he' going to be a legend in his time," said Bill.

"Hell, he's already a legend, I just yesterday bought the fifth book about his bounty hunting exploits, I read in the newspaper that his books have surpassed Jesse James in sales."

Esau stared blankly at Sam. "I wish they would quit printing that crap."

"Have ya'll done had breakfast?" asked Sam.

"Yeah, afore you ever got out'ta bed," replied Bill.

"What'cha gon'na do now?"

"Well," said Esau, "I'm gon'na see when the stage will connect with the train in Tucumcari so I won't have to lay over there."

"I'll find out for'ya," said Bill.

"Where ya'going?" asked Sam.

"Kansas City."

"Oh."

They all got up to leave, Sam said to take care. Esau went through the hotel lobby and up to his room. Bill went to check on the stage and train schedule.

A while later, Esau came down and saw Bill and Sam in the lobby.

"Did ya'get the schedule?"

"Ain't no schedule, have ya'felt that cold wind outside? The stage won't be leaving and they say the train due into Tucumcari tomorrow will have to lay over there, if'n it even makes it."

"What'cha talking about?"

"A telegraph wire what just come in says a northerner is blowing up, and we're likely ta'be snowed in by tomorrow.— You have felt that cold wind blowing, ain't'ya?"

"Naugh, the love in my heart for my nun keeps me warm."

"If'n I didn't know'ya real good Esau, that would make me sick," said Sam.

"Guess we'll just have'ta hunker down here," Bill said. "And wait it out. I hope it's not like the one about this time back in 65."

Esau and Sam looked unknowing at Bill.

"Let's have some coffee," said Esau.

As the trio set at the table drinking coffee, Esau sitting by the window, noticed a man bundled up in a heavy coat, get off his horse and tie it to the rail. He couldn't help but notice that the horse was a fine strong sorrel with quality lines. He saw the man take his saddlebags off the horse, put them over his shoulder, and come in to the hotel lobby. Shortly the man came into the restaurant, looked around at the empty room, and approached their table.

"Do one of you gents know where the proprietor of the hotel might be?"

"Oh yes, that's me," Bill said." I guess my desk clerk is missing. I'm very sorry. Are you in need of a room?"

"Yes, I am—but first, how could I get a cup of that coffee?"

"Agnes!!" Bill yelled as he got up and pulled up a chair.. "She will be here right away. Why don't you join us."

"Sure, why not," he laid his saddlebags on the floor by the chair, pulled off his heavy coat and hung it on a nearby coat rack.

"My name is Bill Carson—"

The Marshall extended his hand, "I'm Sam Logan."

"And I'm Jones," Esau shook his hand. "What's your name?"

"Brown—Joe Brown."

During this exchange Agnes had set another cup and filled them all.

"Why is this fine looking restaurant empty," Joe asked.

"Just the time of day," Bill said. "Come supper time you won't be able to stir'em with a stick."

Joe Brown did not know he was sitting with the Marshall because his coat was covering his badge. And he also did not know that Jones was a celebrated bounty hunter who could spot an outlaw at forty paces, and who was very curious as to who the initials C.C. stood for in the corner of Joe's saddlebags.

"Where ya'headed for Joe?" Esau asked, "There's bad weather coming."

"Yeah, I know, I'm trying to beat it south. I been riding hard from Pueblo for two days, but I've got to stop and sleep in a bed for a night. Hope I can beat the snow to the Rio Grande valley, then it won't be so bad down through the valley to El Paso."

Joe Brown got up, retrieved his heavy coat, and picked up his saddlebags.

"I noticed a livery stable coming in. I'm going to take my hoss back there and I'll be back to rent the room from'ya, Bill."

"Okay Joe, pleased to help'ya."

After Joe left, Esau nudged Sam and spoke to Bill.

"Bill, Sam and I will be back for supper. We're going down to his office for a spell."

"Okay, I believe were having some more of them good winter greens and fried corn pawn."

"Sounds good Bill," Esau said as they went out the door.

In the Marshall's office after hearing Esau's suspicions, Sam was going through old stacks of wanted posters looking for a name with the initials C.C.

Jake Evans, the only deputy on duty at the office spoke up.

"Ain't but one man with them initials Boss. That's Cheyenne Cooper. He's been unheard of for nigh-on to three years now. You remember his gang was wiped out by a bunch of organized lawmen down near Las Cruces. They were trying to make it to their winter refuge in Ciudad Juarez, across the river from El Paso. The whole gang was wiped out except for Cheyenne. He was never found."

"Oh yeah, I remember that gang. They terrorized Nebraska, Wyoming and Colorado, robbing banks and trains. I remember that up in Idaho they, in a period of one year, robbed the same train four times."

"They were vicious killers too," said the deputy.

"Here it is, I found it, the wanted poster, Cheyenne Cooper, $10,000. dollars, dead or alive."

"You want ta'go over to the hotel and get'em Boss?"

"No, this one belongs to Esau. If he hadn't seen the clues, we would never have know about him.—You want'ta go get him now, Esau."

"Naugh, he'll wait till morning. Let's go eat some supper."

"Good idea."

Sam and Esau met up with Bill in the hotel lobby. Bill had a table waiting.

As they sat down to eat, Agnes was putting a bowl of turnip greens and a bowl of big lima beans on the table.

Esau saw Cheyenne come through the door from the hotel lobby. He saw his face pale as he looked directly at the badge on Sam's coatless chest. Cheyenne abruptly turned, went back through the lobby, out the door, and turned toward the livery stable. As he passed the restaurant door, Esau went out onto the walk and called to him.

"Cheyenne! Hold up!"

He turned while drawing his sidearm. As his pistol came into firing line, Esau had no choice. Fast as lightening he drew and put two slugs into Cheyenne's chest. Esau stepped up close to him as he lay on his back and looked up toward him through weakening eyes and faintly spoke. "Jones?——Esau Jones?" He took his last breath and was dead.

Esau thought, only momentarily, of Mother Angelina's statement about making a living that didn't require killing people. *"What the hell,"* he thought. *"It was kill or be killed."*

Chapter 9

Early morning in Marshall Sam Logan's office. Esau signed his book for the $10,000. bank draft.

"Esau, I'll put notice of Cheyenne's demise on the wire so it will be picked up by the newspapers. I'll give a two week notice for his body to be claimed. If it is not he will be buried in the state pen's cemetery, in which case I'll have his hoss corralled at the livery stable for you to pick up. It will help you in getting your hoss farm started."

"I really appreciate that Sam. He is about the finest sorrel I think I've ever seen. He has the true reddish-brown with splashes of yellow coloring. You don't see many of'em with the yellow addition. Yeah Sam, he's a beauty al'right."

"It makes me hope nobody claims ol'Cheyenne, Esau. When are you gon'na be leaving for Las Cruces?—you did say Las Cruces, didn't you?"

"Not till after the bank opens. Might as well have some breakfast."

"I'm game,—watch the store, Jake."

"Sure, Boss."

"I'll be back sometime in the spring for sure to pick up the sorrel."

"You say you're going down through the valley like he was going to do?"

They walked into the restaurant as Esau answered him.

"Yeah, that's the best way. I won't be running into snow in the valley."

"What'cha going to Las Cruces for, Esau?" Sam asked as they sat down.

"So I won't get snowed in here. You know I've got to keep working, and I figure there's probably a lot of outlaws go south for the winter, like ol'Cheyenne was doing. And you know, I know Marshall Sam Pickett there. He might know of some that winter's along the border around there and El Paso."

Bill Carson joined them as Esau talked.

"Well, if you got'ta go, tell Pickett hey for me, he's a good man."

"I'll be sure to do that Sam,—hey, y'all ain't related are'ya?" he laughed.

"I guess we ought ta'be, we're both Samuel's."

"Esau, do you want to take that big heavy coat that Cheyenne left here?"

asked Carson.

"Naugh, I think I can beat the snow to the valley if I leave right away."

They ate breakfast, drink coffee and rambled on until the bank opened. Sam and Bill both walked to the bank with him where he cashed the $10,000. draft and put it in his saddlebag. They walked to the livery stable where he paid his bill, saddled the Bay and said their good-byes. Sam and Bill really hated to see him go. He assured them that he would return in the spring. "After-all," he said. "I have a hoss to pick up."

They, with Esau leading the Bay, walked out of the livery stable into a light snowfall. They went back toward the hotel watching the snowflakes get bigger.

"Bill, I spoze I'll take that big coat. It's nigh most a day's ride afore I reach the valley."

Bill ran into the hotel and came out with the coat while Sam rubbed the Bay's nose.

Esau put the coat on and mounted the Bay. He waved to them and headed out of town going south. Sam and Bill stood in the snow watching him leave like they were losing a family member.

Esau made camp on the downward slope toward the valley. He had left the snow two or three hours back. It was still considerable cold so he left the big coat on when he bunked down for the night. Drifting to the west the next day he came to the Rio Grande around mid-day. After making himself a pot of coffee while the Bay drink his fill of fresh water, he followed the river the rest of the day without incident, except for seeing a few Apache scouts across the river from him. They sat their ponies and watched him for awhile before moving on.

He saw an old Spanish Mission across the river a few miles before reaching the village of San Antonio which he remembered well. The Mission jarred the image of Maria foremost to his mind. And the thought of her still being in that Mission in California. He must hurry and get her away from there before she becomes too accustomed to it and becomes a full-fledged nun. The thought hurt him greatly. He knew he could do nothing about finding a home until the winter was over in Missouri. Until then he must make more money for that purpose. *"I will send her another telegram,"* he said aloud, *"and tell her I love her and will have a home for her, in the Spring."*

Dark was fast approaching and Esau made camp just past the village of San Antonio, a little way above where the infamous redleg massacre occurred. There are still those studious investigators who maintain that it had to be at least three Gatling Guns at work to execute such a feat as was carried out that day on the Rio Grande. The dime novel of Esau Jones, bounty hunter, was the only account that had it right.

Even in the valley the nights were exceptionally cool so Esau laid the big coat over his other cover and slept like a baby. After daybreak he was up making coffee and a little pot of corn meal gruel to eat with a hardtack. He gave the Bay an apple, cleaned his utensils, packed up, tied the big coat with a saddle tie next to his bedroll and was off, following the river.

The third night found him at Hatch. He had made good time this third day, passing two great long lakes where the river had widened out. He made camp knowing that he would be in Las Cruces in another four hours if he kept up the same pace. In the morning he went through the same eating and coffee routine as the previous morning.

About mid-day Esau rode into Las Cruces and went directly to Marshall Sam Pickett's office. The Marshall looked up as Esau entered.

"Esau Jones, hot-dang man, you said you'd come back. I read about that pressing business up the river, and some more pressing businesses too. What brings you to Las Cruces?"

He reached over and shook the Marshall's hand. "It ain't nothing important Sam, it's just too darn cold up north. Thought I'd look around and see if any outlaws might be wintering down this way."

"It's a known fact that Ciudad Juarez is a favorite place for outlaws to lay low during the winter. But they are always coming into the states, and robbing banks and an occasional train, and running right back across the border. They once in awhile hit a bank in New Mexico, but most of their action is in Texas. They also have other hideouts in Mexico too, all along the border. They run back and forth from Texas to the sanctuary of Mexico. A number of years ago the entire gang of an outlaw was killed near here by a bunch of lawmen as they were trying to get back into Mexico below El Paso. You probably don't remember them, their leader got clean away. His name was Cheyenne Cooper. The outlaw gangs that winter in Mexico work the entire south part of Texas, from El Paso, around the Big Bend area, and across to San Antonio and Austin, and south to Laredo. I just heard yesterday about a bank being robbed in Pecos. They aren't sure but it is believed to have been the Billings Kid gang out of Montana. A bank clerk picked the young leader from pictures of bank robbers off the wire."

"Sounds like southern Texas is an outlaw paradise."

"It sure is Esau—if you can catch'em afore they get back into Mexico."

"Or go into Mexico and bring'em back."

"But Mexico is out of our jurisdiction."

"Not mine, Sam. See if you can find a wanted poster on this Billings Kid, and point me to a good eating place. Have you had dinner?"

"Thanks Esau, I ate a little while ago. Go down to the right to the hotel, they have a good restaurant. I'll work on digging out some more probable posters for'ya."

"Thanks Sam," Esau started to the door and turned back. "Oh, Sam Logan said to tell'ya hey," he went out the door and turned toward the hotel with his saddlebags over his left shoulder, leaving the Bay in front of the Marshall's office. After a fine meal and three cups of coffee he went back to the Marshall's office.

"Hey Esau, did'ya have dinner?"

"Yeah, it was real good."

"I picked out about ten likely suspect's for'ya, aside from this here one on that Billings Kid Gang. He's quite a dude, he is. His gang numbers six real mean hombres, all killers," he handed the poster to Esau, "here you look at it." The first thing Esau noticed was $10,000 for Billings and $2,000 for each member of his gang. The six members were listed as Lester McCoy, Wayne W. Slocum, Edward "Beehive" McCallister, Floyd "Buster" Fougerty, Johnny Smith and Paul Comer.

The Billings Kid actual name was Albert Forest. He hailed from Billings, Montana, as did his gang, and was sure enough a youngster and a fancy dresser.

Esau put the posters in his saddlebag.

"I spoze you'll be going down to El Paso?"

"Spoze so, that seems to be the place to start looking."

"Have'ya ever been there?"

"Nope."

"Good luck—if'n you want to check in with the Marshall, his name is Tom Greenstreet, he's a friend of mine and quiet a congenial feller. You'll like him."

He road through a winding sandy downgrade for about three hours and then leveled off straight as an arrow for another three hours before reaching El Paso.

Esau came to El Paso at its peak of becoming a boomtown after the arrival of the Southern Pacific railroad. By 1881 the Texas and Pacific and the Atchison, Topeka and Santa Fe would be completed, and also servicing El Paso. After the end of the Civil War, El Paso had begun to grow and encompassed the small communities that had developed along the Rio Grande. The population boom that Esau was right in the middle of attracted newcomers ranging from Businessmen and Priests, to Gunfighters and Prostitutes. El Paso had become a boomtown known affectionately as "Six Shooter Capital" because of its lawlessness. Prostitution and Gambling flourished.

The main street was busy with cowhands going from one saloon to another. Wagons loaded with building materials. Horse drawn trolleys, and buggies of all descriptions. The town bustled with various activities as new buildings spring up on both sides of the street and onto the next block over. It seemed that every other building was a saloon or a house of pleasure.

Esau slowly rode down the street, fascinated by the commotion, until he saw a bank on a corner next to a mercantile store. He tied the Bay to a hitching rail, took his saddlebags and went into the bank. He waited his turn to see the clerk.

"Is this the closest bank to the Marshall's office?"

"Yes Sir, it is."

"Where is the Marshall's office?"

"It's on the side street right behind the bank, Sir.—How else may I help you?"

"I'd like to open a savings account."

Esau took the cash from his saddlebag from the last two drafts he had cashed. "Twelve thousand cash, Sir." He put five hundred in his pocket to strengthen his living expenses.

"Yes Sir." The clerk counted the money as he spoke. "I'll need your name and address, Sir."

"The name is Esau Jones, the address will in care of the U.S. Marshall's office behind your bank."

The clerk's eyes widened and he became somewhat hyperactive as he made Esau a receipt for his $12,000. "You hang on to your receipt, Mister Jones, It's a pleasure doing business with you, and I'm real pleased to make your acquaintance—Sir."

Esau put the receipt in a side pocket inside his saddlebag and went out the door. He led the Bay around to the Marshall's office.

"Esau Jones, come in here and have a seat," he heard as soon as he stepped through the door. It was Marshal Tom Greenstreet getting up from behind his desk and pushing his hand toward Esau. They shook hands and both sat down.

"Sam Pickett wired me you were coming. He said for me to take good care of you—you know ol' Sam, he said to point'ya to a decent hotel and restaurant. He also said for me to get my jail cells ready and be sure to have plenty leg shackles, he said your outlaws always went barefoot.—I don't know what he meant by that. Sometimes he tries to be funny."

"Yeah, but Sam's a good man—and friend."

"That's for sure."

"Where would I find a livery stable and that decent hotel?"

"Go down this street beside the office. The hotel is on the next corner and the livery is a little further down and across the street. It's beside a Chinese bath house, you can't miss it."

"Thanks Tom, I'll see you later." Esau picked up his saddlebag and went out the door. He knew he would never get over the habit of taking his saddlebags with him everywhere he went.

He gave instructions for the Bay. Clean his hoofs, give him a good currycombing and brushing, and oats twice a day. The liveryman assured him he would be well taken care of. He crossed the busy street with his saddlebags on his left shoulder and came back to the hotel. It, as every good hotel does, had a fabulous restaurant. He rented a room for an undetermined amount of time and went into the restaurant. As has been earlier mentioned, Esau for some reason has a strange magnetism for the outlaw element. It could possibly be because of the signs emitted by their suspicious nature. Just as the three high-strung creeps who came in and sat at the corner table, and were constantly looking around and moving nervously when someone else came in. Esau was somewhat unnoticed with his hat off and sitting where his guns were hidden by the table. The three hombres each ordered a plate of food and coffee, the same as Esau was eating. He inconspicuously kept a keen eye on them. When they got up to leave he took special notice as to how each of them wore his sidearm. As they went out the door Esau got up and put his money by the register and went partly out the door so as to keep an eye on where they were going. They went down the street and crossed over to the livery stable. Esau crossed over from the restaurant and then went toward the livery stable. There were so many people on the street that the trio could not have detected the fact that he was following them. As Esau got to the side of the livery stable, seven men came out leading their horses. Three of them were the hombres from the restaurant.

Esau immediately saw the young duded up Kid come out last and rationalized that it was the Billings Kid. The Kid wore a black suit with a white lacy shirt and black string tie. He wore a derby hat and topped his attire off with large blue and yellow ribbon shoulder-knots sewn on the shoulders of his coat.

Esau stepped up beside the Kid and fast as lightening drew his right hand pistol and cracked him above his right ear while nimbly lifting his pistol with his left hand. He did the same to the man ahead of the Kid before the others were aware of the onslaught. Esau remembered the two that wore their pistols up high and the one gunfighter with his pistol low for a faster draw. He shot him first when they turned on him. Consequently, all five shots that were fired were from Esau's two forty-fives. The shots were so close together they sounded like one loud clap of thunder. Four of the five cleared leather, but lifting their guns to aim lost them valuable time, whereas Esau shot from the hip.

By the time the Billings Kid and Lester McCoy came around nursing severe headaches, the Marshal, Tom Greenstreet and three Deputies were on the scene.

"I tried to bring them all in alive Tom, but they didn't won't to come."

"You did a good job, Esau. I didn't won't to feed all of that bunch anyway. That boy with the funny coat, isn't that the Billings Kid?—they robbed the Pecos bank the other day. I was just yesterday looking at his wanted poster."

"Yeah, me too."

"Man, ol'Sam was sure right about you—You got'ta bunch of money coming for all of them."

"Yeah, twenty-two thousand, a pretty good haul,—beats the hell out of digging taters."

"I'll have my boys to help the undertaker with these five dead ones. Me and you will take these two to my place, and give them a room." Tom turned his attention to his Deputies. "Paul, you and Johnny get a feed wagon from the livery and load these bodies in it for the undertaker. Bring all their gun rigs to the office. Dave, you come with us and put leg shackles on this here feller with the Kid and take him to the undertakers place to identify his dead companions, and put their names on a card, and put it in their shirt pocket so they can get the proper names on the grave markers—Y'all got all that?"

Johnny had removed the five gun belts and he handed them to Dave before he went after the wagon. At the office Dave put the leg shackles on Lester McCoy, got some cards for names and waited awhile to give them time with moving the bodies, before going to the undertaker's parlor. The Marshall, taking no chances, shackled the Kid before locking him in a cell.

"Tom, I'm going to the hotel," Esau said. "I haven't had much sleep lately."

"Okay Esau, I'll make out your money draft in the morning. I'm also going to wire Sam in the morning and let him know you got the Billings Kid and his gang. I'm sure he would like to know it. He's a real good friend, ya'know."

"Yeah, we're good friends too."

"Ya'know—I'd like ta'join that club too."

"Well, I think you've been initiated,—okay, you're in." he laughed.

Marshall Tom Greenstreet, with a big smile of sincerity, like he had been given a spotted puppy, knowingly shook Esau's hand.

Chapter 10

Marshall Tom Greenstreet made out a U.S. Government bank draft to Esau Jones in the amount of $22,000 dollars, bounty payment for Albert Forest, alias The Billings Kid and his six accomplices.

"Tom, breakfast for you and the boys is on me this morning."

"Sounds good to me. Paul, you can go with us, Dave and Johnny, y'all stay here and I'll have y'alls brought over with breakfast for the prisoners."

"They can't go, Tom?"

"It's a standing rule here, Esau, at least one deputy is to be here at all times if we have a prisoner. With these two I fill it best to have two deputies stay."

"I guess it's a good rule Tom, but what say, let's just all stay and have it brought here."

The deputies were all in approval with big smiles. "Alright, boys," Tom said. "Two of y'all go and bring it over here. Get it for the prisoners too, we can make coffee here. I think we have enough cups in the cupboard."

Esau unbuttoned his shirt pocket and took out some Union folding money and handed Paul a one hundred dollar bill.

"You don't have to pay for the prisoners Esau, I'll put theirs on the jail expense."

"That's okay Tom, let me do it just this time."

"Esau," asked Johnny. "Do you ever feel any remorse for killing outlaws?"

"Well, I don't kill them if I can keep from it. I've brought more in alive than I've ever killed. But, as far as feeling remorse——naugh, no more than I would to kill a poisonous snake."

"How many people have you ever killed in a day's time?"

Absent of expression, Esau looked straight into Johnny's eyes, and answered immediately. "Sixty, but they weren't bandits, they were some of them Union Militia's poisonous snakes."

"Johnny," Tom spoke harshly. "You shouldn't ought'ta be asking such questions of Esau."

"It's alright Tom, I don't mind," said Esau with a grin.

Paul, Dave and two Chinamen came in with three pots of food, plates, silverware, cloth napkins, and salt and pepper. After the Chinamen had left the talk got around to why there were so many Chinese in about every town across the nation. The further west you went the more there were. Tom seemed the most knowledgeable on the subject so he lead the conversation and told them about the Chinese coming to this country on about every imaginative kind of ship afloat to work in the gold fields after the discovery of gold at Sutter's Mill in 1849. Large gold mining companies sent representatives to China to hire the people to work for them in the placer deposits. They worked the rivers and streams by the thousands. "Once the placer locations had been depleted," Tom said. "The Chinese were displaced to about every major town in the west to find work. They on a whole are a very enterprising people. Many started businesses of their own like laundries, bath houses, restaurants and small time gambling halls and whore houses. Others pursued employment as workers in such places. Now you know why there's Chinamen ever where you look."

"Damn Boss," Dave said. "You ought'ta be a school teacher. I never even thought about'em coming from somewhere. They's just here, ya'know, like all the rest of us."

After eating breakfast and having two cups of coffee, Esau got up from a chair at the end of one of the desks, located his hat and announced, as he shouldered his saddlebags, that he was going around to the bank.

He went to the same clerk and deposited the $22,000 dollar draft into his account bringing it up to $34,000. Upon returning to the Marshall's office he told Tom that he came by to let him know that he would be in his room if needed. He was going to get a little more sleep and study the handful of wanted posters which Sam had given him.

Esau put his left hand pistol under his pillow and hung his right hand rig on a wall hook by the dresser. He took the wanted posters from his saddlebag and laid them on the bed. He began to look through them as he slowly removed his boots. With his head laid back on the pillow he read a little about the murderous bank and train robber, "Red Dog", Murdock, before dozing off. He slept all day, awakening near supper time with the thought of winter turnip greens and fried corn pone. He wondered if they might have some here.

He wasn't long in finding out that they didn't. If he ate supper this evening, it would have to be smothered liver and onions with lots of gravy and lumpy mashed potatoes. For bread it was large hand-rolled biscuits. Every table was adorned with a large bottle of pure ribbon cane syrup.

"What the hell," he thought. *"It's better'n eating on the trail."*

It didn't take much for Esau to get his fill. He paid the girl at the register and went back to his room. He hung his pistol rig back up by the mirror, put his other gun under the pillow, and pulled off his boots. He then got serious about studying the posters. To begin with he picked out the ones that had a Ten thousand dollar bounty. The top one was "Red Dog" Murdock, bank and train robber, out of Nebraska with a gang of eight men. The bounty on his men was five hundred dollars each. During the past summer Murdock and his men had robbed the Union Pacific twice, at separate locations. The Union Pacific ran from Chicago to Ogden, Utah and across the Overton Route through Winnemucca, and Reno, Nevada to Sacramento, California where it connected with the Southern Pacific, both north and south.

Red Dog's description was given as a burly, red-complexioned man of middle age, with a bull-dog face, and being as mean as he looked. The poster stated that Red Dog and his gang were expected to be in the southern Texas or Mexico area during the winter. His eight regulars were all men in their thirties, and all killers. They were listed as Nathan Gilmore, Thomas Franklin Washburn, Albert Lincoln, Anthony Pierce, Lester McGinnis, Roy "Big Boy" Sawyer, Benny Benson, and Edward "Boxcar" Lawson.

As Esau started to pick up another wanted poster, there was a light tapping on his door. He reached under his pillow and got his pistol. Holding the pistol behind his back, he unlocked the door and opened it slightly. At the door was a young Mexican girl. He looked down the hall, both ways, and motioned her in. He locked the door and asked her how she got by the desk clerk. Esau knew she was a prostitute, but he also knew they were not allowed to solicit in this hotel.

"I watched carefully until he went into the restaurant, and I slipped up the stairs. I saw you go into this room earlier, and you looked like a man who needed companionship."

The girl spoke very good English. When Esau asked her about it, she said she had gone to school in Socorro, Texas, where her parents live, and since it is in the U.S. they taught both English and Spanish.

"I do not wish your services, not because I wouldn't like to, you are a very attractive young lady. But you see, I am engaged to another beautiful young lady and, it just wouldn't be right to her."

"I understand, that's very commendable of you, I'm sorry I wasted your time."

"No, No, don't be sorry, in fact I would like it if you would stay and talk for awhile. I'll be glad to pay for your time. How much do you normally make for a couple of hours?"

"Over at Alfonso's,—the hotel where I normally work, at five dollars a man I only make about thirty or forty dollars a night, and the boss takes most of that. That's because of all the competition. It seems like all the women in El Paso wants to be a whore. The boss sends me over here occasionally because the people that stay here will pay more. I usually get as much as fifteen dollars here, or twenty for the whole night. I've been hoping things would get better so I can help out my Mama and Papa, but it never looks like it will."

Esau looked at her in disbelief. He remembered a time back in Omaha when he shelled out forty bucks.

"What is your name?" asked Esau.

"Maria.—And I'm twenty two years old."

Esau had a sudden rush and felt ill. With a motionless and paled face he stared at her. *"This,"* thought Esau, *"But for the grace of God, and Rosa—could be my Maria."*

"You want to hear something strange.—My betrothed is also named Maria. I believe she is about twenty five now."

"Where is she. Is she Mexican?"

"She is a Spanish Baroness, and she lives in a convent in California."

There was absolute silence for what seemed like an eternity.

"Yes." Esau said. "She is a nun."

After more silence the girl spoke slowly and coherently. "Let's see now, you are engaged to a nun in California,—and you are a gunslinger in Texas. I assumed you were a gunslinger from the way you wear that rig hanging by the dresser. And like most gunslingers you are between jobs. Am I right?"

"Yeah, on most counts.—I am between jobs and I'm engaged to a nun, but I'm not a gunslinger. I'm a bounty hunter."

"Just about the same thing, I would think.—Have you ever had sex with your Maria? Do you have a name?"

"No, not yet.—My name is Esau Jones."

"Esau?" That's a strange name."

"Yeah, my mama gave it to me. It's from the bible. She told me that the bible said Esau was a great hunter."

"Are you a great hunter, Esau?"

"Some folks seem to think so.—Listen, beings how you meet a lot of men, tell me, have you ever heard of a man that goes by the name of Red Dog Murdock?"

"Yeah, he's an outlaw. I've never met him, but I know two men that ride with him. Lester and Albert, They are regular customers at Alfonso's. They always ask for me."

"Could you describe them for me?"

"Sure, they are about thirty, well built, and always in need of a shave. I see them at the same time.—Not together, you know, but one after the other, about once a week. One sure way you can tell them is by their hat. They both wear black hats with a silver concho hatband."

Esau took some twenty dollar bills from his pants pocket. "Here's twenty dollars you can tell your boss you got for the night." He counted off five more twenties. "And here is one hundred for you."

"You are too gracious Senor. Now I can go help out my poor Mama and Papa in Socorro. Are you sure you don't want me before I go Senor Esau. I really don't believe you will ever get none from your nun.—That's why they call them nuns you know."

"Thanks anyway, but I will wait."

"Then adios Senor, I wish the best for you and your Maria."

Esau opened and looked out the door. He motioned an all clear for her and she quietly disappeared down the hall.

Esau lay back down and tried to clear his head. *"God,"* he thought. *"What a talker. I sure hope the hell my Maria is not as talkative as that one. It would drive me crazy."* He suddenly sat back up and put his boots on. He could see by the window that it was breaking dawn outside, and he did not want to go to sleep. He planned on having breakfast in about an hour and he wanted to talk to the Marshal, after which he intended on going to the Chinese bath house for a good scrubbing and a clean shave. He picked up the next poster and began to read it.

Ten Thousand dollar reward dead or alive for Sam Johnson alias "Minnesota Sam" racketeer, extortionist. He is wanted on twelve counts of protective insurance extortion throughout Minnesota, Iowa, and Kansas, including two counts of murder in Iowa. He is believed to be in southern Texas or Mexico for the winter months. Approach him with caution. Sam Johnson is in his fifties, graying sideburns and mustache, clean cut and dresses exceedingly well, but somewhat modest, in suit and tie. He wears a derby hat and conducts himself with refined elegance.

Esau walked to the Marshall's office to have a chat with Tom and see if he was up to some breakfast.

"Sure, I was hoping you'd come by.—Watch the office boys, I'll be back in a little while."

"Okay boss." Johnny said. "Hi Esau, How are you this fine morning?"

"I'm feeling just great, Johnny."

They walked up the street to the restaurant and went in through the hotel lobby. After ordering breakfast Esau asked Tom how many outlaws he could handle at the jail.

"Why Esau, are you about to bring in some more?"

"Could be, I'm not sure yet but I've got a lead on "Red Dog" Murdock and eight followers."

"Holly crap Esau, are they in town?"

"Two of his men are. If I play my cards right they will lead me to him, sometime within a week. I believe it's in the works now.—Can you handle nine or should I kill some of them?"

Tom Greenstreet stared bewilderedly at Esau.

"Don't get your drawers in a huff Tom, I was only kidding. You know I wouldn't shoot any more than I absolutely have to.—So, can you take the whole lot of'em?"

"With the two we have, that's eleven. Putting two to the cell, I can handle eight and put three over at the Sheriffs jail, he has two cells, if he is empty.—Hell, perhaps you better just kill about three of'em."

"Okay, if you say so." They both laughed.

As a spur of the moment decision, Esau decided to go see about the Bay and let him know he hadn't deserted him. As he started into the livery a shot rang out just as Esau felt the spiral of a bullet whiz by his ear, and the hollow thud, as it buried deep into a six by six door stanchion. He instinctively dove and rolled into the stable and behind the wall. Looking through a crack in the wall he saw the sun reflect on a gun barrel as it was pulled behind the curtain of an upstairs window across the street. The name on the establishment was Al's Pleasure House. Getting his bearings as to the location in regard to the front door, he quickly went out the back and ran down the alley, crossed the street and came back up to the establishment staying close to the inside of the walk. Two steps at a time he bolted up the stairs and kicked the door in, shooting the man that turned on him with his gun drawn. He put four quick shots in the chest of the man in the black hat with silver conchos. He was the only one in the room except the whore Maria whom had been beaten severely and was sobbing uncontrollably. Being the talker that she was, Esau knew she would reveal his presence and plans. He just didn't know it would be so soon. Not knowing where the other black hat with the silver hatband was, he had to assume that he was off to tell "Red Dog" the state of affairs.

Someone had called the Sheriff who came in as Esau was trying to console Maria. Esau told him what happened and said he had to leave to try and intercept the other man. Through the Marshall, the Sheriff knew of Esau and his dilemma with bringing in outlaws. He told Esau to go ahead, that he would call Tom. Esau said to tell Tom that the dead man is one of "Red Dog" Murdock's men.

Esau went and quickly saddled the Bay. He told the livery man he would be back, and gave him a one hundred dollar bill to put on his account, and ask him where the bridge to Mexico was. He was only about fifteen minutes from it. Esau intended on sitting up a secret surveillance at the bridge to watch for the other black hat, coming or going, and follow him to his boss.

Chapter 11

Esau found a good place where he would not be noticed and got off of the Bay, when to his amassment he spotted the bandit in the black hat headed across the bridge. He didn't know how, but he had gotten ahead of him. With the man just getting to the bridge meant that he probably knew of his companion's demise. Esau mounted the Bay and followed at a safe distance. When he came off the bridge Esau noticed the Federally border guards huddled in conversation while looking at him. He did not have far to go. The man in the black hat stopped by an establishment made of clapboard and stucco. It seemed to be a saloon and boarding house combined. The entire town was made up of many such places and a conglomeration of shacks and shanties, with kids, pigs and chickens running amuck.

The man in the black hat with the silver concho hatband, put his horse in a corral with seven other horses, all saddled. He then went inside the establishment.

Esau rode back to the bridge and stopped to talk with the Federally border guards. They were quite amiable and addressed him graciously as Senor Esau. One of them held out a Spanish copy of his first book and sprightly mimicked shooting a Gatling gun. Fortunately one of the guards (the Capitan) could almost speak English.

"Senor Esau, my compadres are happy to acquaint with you." Esau smiled and gave them the high sign. They mimicked it with big smiles.

"Yes, you are a hero—do you pursue the bad man which you followed."

"Yes, there are more of them in that place." Esau motioned to the establishment as he answered. The Capitan caught his companions up on the talk.

"Si," they all answered as they held up nine fingers.

"Will you be taking them back across the border?"

"Yes, if I can figure out a way to do it."

The Capitan spoke to his comrades. They whole-heartedly agreed with whatever it was that he said.

"Senor Esau, we will be grateful to assist you. What shall we do?—You will give instruction? Yes."

"Yes,—You and your men will arrest them and put their pistoles and rigs into a feed sack."

"Feed sack, si."

"Tie their hands behind their backs."

"Si, tie the hands."

Esau was going through the motions as he explained the procedure. "Then we will take the right hand bridle off of their hosses and tie it into a left side saddle ring.—I will show you when we get there. We are going to make a caravan with them tied on to their horses. We will take off their boots and tie their feet into the stirrups. When I leave with the caravan of bad men, I will let you keep their pistoles and boots for some needy amigos."

The Capitan explained the plan to his compadres. They were gleeful, and all hugged Esau. At the break of day the following morning the plot was carried out without incident. The soldiers brought the sleeping men from the rooms under restraint of nudging with rifle barrels. They brought them all together. Some had put on their pants and some only had on long-johns. The soldiers gathered their pistol rigs and boots in three feed sacks. All of the outlaws had put on their hats. Cowboys have trouble moving without their hat on. Esau related directions through the Capitan. He told them to find the saddlebags and put them on the horses in the corral and put their clothes in another feed sack and tie it on one of their hosses. He gave them leather straps from his saddlebags to tie their hands securely behind their backs. They then marched them out to the corral and helped them onto the saddles. He showed them how to tie one end of the removed half of the bridle into a saddle tie. He gave the soldiers more leather straps to tie their feet into the stirrups. They then lined the horses up going out the gate and tied the half of the bridle from each horses bit to the end of the bridle from the saddle tie of the horse in front creating his caravan similar to the one he made of rope for the Double-Bar-M cattle rustlers..Esau individually thanked and shook the hand of each Federally border guard, re-checked all of the connections, found a lasso rope and tied one end into the halter of the lead horse and wrapped it around the Bays saddle horn.

"Senor Esau, we will watch for more bad men, you drop-over often and check-up with—or visit us, Si?"

"Si." Esau mounted the Bay, and led his grumbling and disinclined caravan of outlaws across the bridge and up the main drag to the El Paso Marshals office. On the way he gathered a large crowd of hilariously curious spectators. Marshal Tom Greenstreet, and Deputy Johnny stood momentarily in a state of mental paralysis, on the walkway in front of the office, as Esau, his caravan and onlookers stopped in front of them.

"Well, I be damned," Tom muttered. "Sam Pickett said he'd be bringing'em in barefooted. He didn't say nothing about bringing'em in naked."

"Hey Tom, I brung'ya ol' Red Dog and his men, cept for one I shot over at that Al's place."

"Yeah, he's at the morgue being cleaned up and measured. I guess that there real ugly one is Red Dog Murdock."

"Yeah, I reckon so."

"Boss," Johnny said. "We ain't got room for all of them."

"What we'll have ta'do Johnny, is shackle them in the prisoner transfer car down yonder on the sidetrack. It will be picked up next week to go to the Federal Prison in Bastrop. We can put them two in our jail in the prisoner car too."

"What kind of prison is that in Bastrop?" asked Esau, who had gotten off the Bay and was standing on the walk with them.

"It's a maximum security prison where they will be processed and live awaiting trial or transfer to other places for trials."

"Where is this Bastrop?"

"About thirty miles southeast of Austin. The transfer car on the sidetrack is a special built maximum security car for hauling prisoners. When we get a whole gang of prisoners we shackle and chain them in the seats. The prisoner car is equipped with shackles and chains, but we have to furnish four guards to travel with them. They will then return on the next train coming west. We have four men who are deputized and hire out just for that job.

"Why didn't you mention that when we talked about killing some of them so you could have enough room to jail them?"

"I didn't think of the prisoner car, or I wanted to see if you really wanted to kill some of them, or I thought I'd wait to see if you would really be bringing them in—or,—where the hell are their boots and clothes?"

"Their clothes are in a sack tied on one of their hosses— they didn't have any boots, or guns. You need to check their saddlebags. I have not looked in them."

Tom opened his door and called,—Dave!—Paul!—y'all come out here! We've got work to do!" He turned back to Esau. "Do you know how much the bounty comes to?"

"Fourteen thousand.—Ten for Red Dog and four for the eight men. That's including the dead one."

"Johnny," Tom said. "Go over to the Sheriff's office and see if he can round up a couple of part time deputies to help us shackle these prisoners in the rail car and stand guard for the night with two of my deputies. Then we will make arrangements tomorrow for the rest of the week."

"Okay, Boss."

"What can I do Tom?" asked Esau.

"You can go over to the hotel restaurant with me and have some dinner. Then we will come back and make your draft so you can get it to the bank before it closes.—I'll leave Dave and Paul in charge of this. They are very capable men."

"Okay, sounds good, I sure need some coffee."

"These are sure some grungy men, where did'ya find'em at?"

"Down in Mexico.—Tell your men to take precaution, they are as dangerous as they are grungy."

"How the hell did you bring them across the border?"

"T'weren't no problem, Tom," he stuck out his chest and tried to put on an air of importance. "I'm a hero, ya' know,— I've got friends and admirers everywhere I go."

Tom looked un-amused at Esau. "Yeah, you're right, you need some coffee."

Marshall Tom Greenstreet looked in wonder at the four fried eggs and steak that Esau ordered for dinner.

"Well, I didn't have any breakfast and I can't remember if I ate supper yesterday."

"I didn't say anything," said Tom.

The waitress brought out Tom's plate of three eggs and steak. The two men looked at it, and at one another.

"I didn't say anything," said Esau.

When finished eating, they went back to the Marshal's office and Tom made the draft for Esau. Esau signed his book for payment and went to the bank where he deposited it bringing his account up to $48,000. While the clerk was logging the deposit, Esau was watching, through a glass partition, a distinguished looking man consulting with the bank president in his enclosed office. The man was showing Mister Glover, the president, some papers and was from all indication, with pen in hand, cajoling him to sign them. Esau immediately took note of the graying sideburns and mustache plus the modest clothing attire. He opened the door and went in.

"Mister Glover, this man is a swindler and insurance extortionist. His name is Sam Johnson, better known by his kind as Minnesota Sam." Sam started to put his hand under his coat. Esau quickly drew his left handed pistol from under his belt. "If that hand goes under your coat Sam, you will be a dead man. Now you hold them out away from you so I can plainly see them." Esau reached under Sam's coat and pulled out a .44 caliber Smith and Wesson revolver. He put the pistol under his own belt, and one handedly patted Sam down, coming up with a small .38 caliber derringer, which he pocketed.

"What was he selling you Mister Glover"

"A really good deal on a protective insurance policy."

I'm sure it wasn't near as good as it seemed." Esau said. "If you ever filed a claim against it, you would find that it was worthless."

"That's why it required the premium of the first year in advance."

"What was the price for a year?"

"Eight hundred dollars.—I really feel like an idiot."

"Don't feel bad about it. He has taken the entire midwest with this scheme. I'm gon'na take him over to visit with Tom."

"I don't know how to thank you enough Mister Jones?"

"Don't bother yourself about it. I'm just glad I came in when I did."

Esau nudged Sam Johnson with his pistol. "Let's go Sam."

They walked out and to the corner. "Sam, we turn left here. I want you to walk in front of me to the Marshal's office, and if you get a fancy to run, just remember one thing. I have no qualms about shooting a man in the back.

When they walked through the door Esau said. "Tom, I brought you some company."

"Why have you got that pistol on him?"

"I figured you might want to lock him up."

"Who is he, Esau?"

"He's called Minnesota Sam."

Tom jumped up from his chair. "Holy crap!"

"Do you have the others on the train car?"

"It's being taken care of, you don't give us enough time in between booking prisoners. I'll take this one over there later."

'What's the tab on him?"

"Ten thousand," Esau reached into his saddlebag and found the wanted poster. "Here's the poster on him."

The Marshal put the poster on his desk. "Can we do this in the morning, Esau?"

"Sure,—soon as you lock him up, I'm gon'na go get some sleep. I'm running kind of short on it lately."

It wasn't yet dark when Esau went to sleep and he awakened to a bright sunny day. After two cups of hot black coffee he went to the Marshalls office. He was welcomed by Deputy Johnny sitting on the bench in front of the office. Johnny got up and opened the door for him.

"Have you had breakfast yet," was Tom's welcome.

"Nope, just coffee."

Tom handed him the draft for $10,000. "Sign my book and I'll buy you're breakfast. All of the prisoners have been fed and my other two men are baby-sitting them along with two from the Sheriff's office."

Esau signed the book. "Okay, I'm hungry as a bear."

While they ate, Tom told Esau he wanted him to not bring him anymore prisoners for awhile. He said they were being over-loaded and over-worked.

ESAU JONES Bounty Hunter

"You're just too good at your work. You need to slow down.—I tell ya'what,—there are Marshall's at Presidio, Fort Stockton, Del Rio, Fredericksburg, Laredo, San Antonio, Austin and Fort Worth. And this time of the year there are a whole passel of wanted men in southern Texas. Why don't you check them places out for a while?—it ain't that we don't like you, Esau. Hell, we love you like a brother." The scrupulous look Esau gave Tom made him open up. "Okay Esau,—well, what it really is—Me and Sam Pickett talked about it on the telegraph and from something he heard, we believe the big boss in Austin may be thinking that we are helping you bring in outlaws and getting a kick-back on the bounty money paid to you.. He don't know that you don't need help, like we know it. Sam says there is talk of maybe an impending investigation."

Esau took a long thoughtful drink of coffee. "Don't let it fret you Tom, I understand your predicament. Probably if I move further east and keep bringing in an unusually large number of outlaws, your boss will see the light. Ya'know,— Austin may be a good place to start, then your boss could study me first hand."

Esau cashed the ten thousand dollar draft, closed his account and left with fifty-eight thousand dollars cash in his saddlebags. He still had plenty subsistence money in his pockets.

After clearing his account at the livery, saddling the Bay, and wishing all the best, he set out for Austin. He knew he could have taken the train which went to San Antonio, and went horseback from there to Austin, but he wanted to see the country. Following the Rio Grande south until early afternoon, and using the position of the sun as a compass, he left the river and headed due east.

His first stop for the night was at a village stage stop called Sierra Blanca. There were only two rooms which were taken by some people waiting on the stage. Others were bunked out in the office and café where meals were served according to what was cooked for the day. This night it was "wrangler stew" and warmed up biscuits. Esau passed on it and went out to water the Bay at a watering trough. He found a place near a feed shed beside the corral and made down his bedroll with the Bay tied on a loose rope next to him. Come morning Esau went back inside and had some coffee before heading on to the east.

For the next two days and one night Esau saw nothing but rolling hills and sagebrush. He arrived at Fort Stockton about sundown. Introducing himself, the Fort's General feed him and put him up for the night. He also had the Bay attended to, and warned Esau of renegade Indians between the Fort and Fredericksburg. He told him it was a full day to the Pecos river, and if he camped there to not use any fire and to stay low. Another half day will be the stage stop at Ozana, and he could use that as his point of no return. If he made it to Ozona the Indian possibilities would lessen for the next day and a half when he would reach Fredericksburg.

The distance had gone as the General had explained. Esau was lucky he didn't see any Indians. He made a pact with himself that it would be a cold day in hell before he ever again rode horseback across Texas. And he wasn't even yet across it. Eight days and he still had two long days before reaching Austin. He fussed and cussed with himself for not taking the train to San Antonio.

In Fredericksburg Esau had left the sagebrush and prairie grass behind and began to see stands of green trees. He visited with the Marshal and got some new wanted posters from him, before finding a livery stable for the Bay to be cleaned, checked and brushed. It was only mid-day when he checking into the nearest hotel, where he had some dinner and retired to his room to study the posters, and get a good night's sleep.

Chapter 12

Another two days found Esau in the big bustling city of Austin, Texas. After finding his way, he went in to see the Commanding officer in charge of all U.S. Marshal's, Captain Barry Battle. Captain B.B. as known by his immediate Marshal's and Deputies, was thoroughly surprised yet delighted to meet the noted Bounty hunter, Esau Jones. They talked at length about Esau's escapades as a bounty hunter and as a raider with Quantrill during the war. Nothing was said that would contribute anything to the validity of the supposed transgression feared by Tom and Sam.

"Tom Greenstreet, in El Paso, is sending a whole parcel of bandits to Bastrop, that I left with him." Esau figured if there was anything to it, B.B.s answer should give him a clue as to its validity.

"They've already arrived.—you've done a marvelous job in El Paso and Las Cruces both. I commend you on your professionalism."

"So much for that." Esau thought.

"By the way, Esau, if you're interested, we've been having a heap of trouble with robberies in the Laredo area, more-so than anywhere else. There are four known gangs playing havoc within a two hundred mile radius of Laredo, on the U.S. side of the river. I have a Marshal and three deputies in Laredo and I have sent troops down there on two occasions, but they take refuge in Nuevo Laredo, in Mexico where they can't get to them. We almost had one of the gangs a while back when my men trailed them, after the Crystal City bank was hit, to Eagle Pass where a gun battle ensued and they got across the river to Piedras Negras. Two of my men were wounded, but not seriously. The Marshal's name down there is Phillip Hancock. Go in and make yourself known. If you go, that is."

"Can you furnish me with wanted posters on the gangs? And can I get a train to Laredo? I have rode hossback across Texas as much I won't to."

"You'll have to change trains in San Antonio, and yes, I'll get the newest lowdown for'ya on the gang's right now."

He pulled out a stack of posters from his bottom desk drawer and went through them, handing Esau four of them. They each consisted of four or five pages.

"You take the best of care, these men are all killers."

"Yes, I will.—but first I must get some sleep if you will point me toward a hotel with a nearby livery."

"That's easy, the livery is to the left about a hundred yards, and the hotel is across the street from it."

Esau put the posters in his saddle bag, thanked the Captain and went out the door. He led the Bay to the livery and told the man to take good care of him, and to give him a bucket of oats. He then crossed the street to the hotel and took a room upstairs with the window facing the street.

The first poster was a twelve man gang made up of war-time Union sympathizers from upstate Kansas, led by a former Redleg Lieutenant, Nathan Donovan, and known widely as the Buck Donovan gang. The bounty on Donovan was $8,000 and $1,000 for each of his men, dead or alive. Esau relished the word dead when he saw that the leader was an ex-redleg.

This was the third year in a row that the Nathan Donovan gang had wintered in the vicinity of Laredo and harassed the complete southern tip of Texas. During the rest of the year they were prevalent through Texas, Oklahoma, Arkansas, Mississippi, Alabama, Tennessee and Kentucky, as bank and train robbers. Although they were known to have robbed mercantile and grocery stores as well as a traveling carnival and side show, where one of the gang shot and killed the bearded lady, thinking she was a man. They preyed on the southern states where the people were Confederate at heart and still followed the traditional southern customs. They would often ride through a small town or community shooting it up like it was still wartime. This gang, the poster stated, is notoriously clever in keeping law enforcement incognizant of their actions, although some of their jobs seemed to be made by a spur-of-the-moment decision. The poster went on to list the names of known members of the gang. Esau did not recognize any of them.

The next wanted poster Esau looked at was for the Dollar Gang, a gang of four dangerous desperados wanted for waylaying and robbing mining payroll couriers. By name they are Olan Dollar, Otis Dollar, Argus Black, and Edwin Sawyer. They ride excellent stalwart mounts in three red Roans and a Buckskin. The government bounty of $3,000 each, matched by the El Dorado Silver Mining Syndicate, comes to $6,000 for each man, dead or alive. They have robbed payrolls at random for almost a full year from seven working mines. The wanted poster was updated to dead or alive after the killing of a payroll courier and four guards in August of this year. The mines lie in a radius of several miles in the vicinity of Barksdale, Camp Wood, Concan and Sabinal, with the smelter being at Uvalde. Payroll in U.S. currency and gold coins is delivered to each mine by a horseback courier and six armed guards, once every month. The Dollar brothers carry the name of the gang but it is believed that plans and decisions are equally shared by all.

As is with all good hotels, Esau had seen a restaurant downstairs when he checked in. With his pistols in place, and his saddlebag slung over his left shoulder he went in to see about some coffee and hopefully a bite to eat, although it was only mid-afternoon. The cook fried him three eggs, which he ate with some warmed-up pan bread, along with three cups of coffee.

The next wanted poster he studied back in his room was about the Nathan Montgomery gang. The gang consisted of eight men including Nathan who were widely known throughout Texas as professional and effective train robbers. With the conglomerate of railroad lines throughout eastern and southern Texas, the Ethan Montgomery gang had not to leave Texas to sustain their chosen profession.

The Southern Pacific Railroad, and Southern Pacific Company, simply called Southern Pacific (1865-1885) acquired the Central Pacific Railroad by lease and grew into a major railroad system which incorporated many smaller companies, such as the Southwestern Railway (Cotton Belt) and the Texas and New Orleans Railroad, and Morgan's Louisiana and Texas Railroad which extended from New Orleans through Texas to El Paso, across New Mexico and through Tucson, to Los Angeles, and throughout most of

California. The Cotton Belt, is the most famous of Southern Pacific's subsidiaries. SP owned many other lines like the Northwestern Pacific, the Southern Pacific Railroad of Mexico, and a variety of narrow gauge routes.

The Nathan Montgomery gang was known strictly as a year round Texas gang. The government bounty was $10,000 on Nathan Montgomery and $1,000 each on the other seven men, and matched equally by Southern Pacific, Dead or Alive.

If by chance Esau could bring them to justice. It would be the biggest single bounty of his career. A total of $34,000.00 dollars.

The day was creeping up toward sundown when Esau awoke from a two hour nap and decided to go down and get a bite of supper. Once in the lobby the notion hit him to see about the Bay before it got dark. When he neared the stable it amazed him to see four such fine horses, left in the corral, with their saddles still on them. His amazement turned to undeniable delight when he saw that the horses were three red Roans and a Buckskin.

After briefly seeing that the Bay was okay, Esau, with a bit of finesse, tactfully questioned the livery attendant.

"Sure is some fine looking hosses out in your corral."

"Yep, sure is."

"Who ever's riding'em must be gon'na leave during the night, what with the saddles left on'em."

"Yep, most likely they are, they just come in about an hour ago."

"You probably wouldn't know where they went?"

"Yep, I sure do, Mister Esau. Stead'of beating around the bush whyn't ya'just ask me?"

"So much for my finesse." Esau thought.

"Are they some kind of outlaws, Mister Esau? I had a sneaking suspicion bout'em cause they acted peculiar and jittery. They left here with a grain sack bout half full of something and tied up. Giving in to my naturally spicious nature I had to follow'em, at a safe distance, ya'know."

"Where did they go?"

"Well, the place ain't real far from here. It's back two streets behind where we're sitting, at bout the biggest gambling parlor in Austin. But Mister Esau, what's funny bout it is that Harvey Salinger, the owner of the place came out in a little while with the same grain sack. I followed him secretly from the other side of the street. He could have never spotted me cause there was a lot of people on the street. Anyway, guess what, he took the grain sack into the bank just as the bank was closing. After bout fifteen minutes he come out without the sack and went back to his establishment and I come back here. Ya'know, I'm sure glad you came, I been bout to bust to tell somebody bout this. Do ya'think they might be some kind'a outlaws."

"How long have you been back here?"

"I had only just got back when you showed up. I hurried to get back before it got dark."

"Then they could be getting here any time now."

"Or they could be gambling, or with a whore. He has rooms and whores."

"Did you notice how they were fixed for guns?"

"Yes Sir, there are carbines on each hoss, and they pack the old ball and cap Army colts. Them things can put a ball plum through'ya."

"Okay listen,—what's your name?"

"My name's Arthur."

"Okay, listen Arthur, they are outlaws, and I know who they are. It's best if we wait right here for them. I don't want to approach them where there are a lot of people that could get hurt. I want you to stand at the edge of the doorway and watch for them while I get the carbines from off the hosses. Don't get out in the moonlight. Stay in the dark and don't light any lamps. I'll be right back and then I won't you to hide out of sight and be quiet."

"Yes Sir, that's the part I like best."

Esau went into the corral and took the carbines from their holsters and loosened the saddle cinches underneath the four horses. He took the carbines into the stable and put them behind some stacked hay. He had Arthur show him which way the men would come from and then told him to hide. *"Good"* he thought. *"They will have to pass by the door."*

Remembering The Billings Kid, and how he subdued him and one of his men at the livery stable in El Paso, he wondered if the same chicanery might possibly work here. He would very soon find out, for they were coming toward the livery.   Esau stood behind the edge of the door in the dark as they stopped in front of the door.

"Olan, the livery boy must have gone home, it's dark as a dungeon in there."

"Yeah, let's just get our hosses and go."

As they started to the corral, Esau stepped out fast as lightening and laid his pistol barrel, with great force, above the last man's right ear, and without hesitation he did the same to the next man in front of that one. An anxious rush of dread overcome the first two men from the vibrant reflection of movement behind them. They both turned and instinctively drew their pistols, causing Esau to draw and fire both of his pistols as one, killing them immediately with shots through their hearts.

Esau took the pistols from the other two and bound their wrists behind them before they revived with excruciating headaches. They turned out to be Olan Dollar and Edwin Sawyer.

While awaiting the Sheriff to investigate the shooting, Esau reloaded his pistols, took the two dead men's pistols, and retrieved his saddlebag from behind the livery stable door.

In a short period of time the Sheriff and two Deputies arrived on the scene. Esau related his story which was confirmed by Arthur. The Sheriff enlisted some help for the deputies to remove the two dead men to the morgue, while he and Esau took the live men to the Marshal's office. Captain B.B. looked up from papers he was studying on his desk.

"Esau got the mining payroll bandits," the Sheriff said. "He had to kill two of'em, here's the other two for you."

A big grin exploded from the Captain's face. "Just like Tom and Sam said, man you sure work fast."

Two deputies, at a signal from the Captain, took the prisoners to the lock-up.

"You were going to Laredo, to hunt these men, and you ain't even left Austin yet." He looked over to the Sheriff. "Where's the two dead ones?"

"My deputies are taking them to the morgue."

"Here's the dead men's pistols." Esau said as he handed two pistols to the Captain.

"Esau, do you want your bounty now or in the morning after the bank opens?"

"In the morning is fine, Captain."

"Yeah, the bank will have to issue the matching bounty, anyway. Twelve and twelve—twenty four thousand.—man-alive Esau, that's quite a haul. What'cha gona do with all that money?"

"I'm go'na add it to the rest of my money, buy me a horse farm, and get married."

"You mean you're gon'na give up bounty hunting?" asked the Captain.

"Yeah, in this business, one can't stay lucky forever."

"When'ya plan on quiting?"

"Sometime in the spring."

"Do you have an expected bride?"

"Yeah, she's out in California."

"You gon'na be living in California?"

"Nope, in Missouri."

"You're staying across the street from the livery, aint;cha?"

"Yep,"

"What'cha say let's meet there for breakfast right after the church bells sound, that'll be at eight o'clock."

"Tomorrow ain't Sunday, is it?"

"Naw, I think it's Tuesday.—The church bells always sound every day at eight o'clock all over town."

"Yeah, breakfast sounds good, I'll be in the restaurant."

After a hearty breakfast with Captain Brady, they walked up the street, in the opposite direction of the livery stable, about another hundred yards to the bank.

The manager cashed the government draft and made a draft on his bank for matching funds of 12,000 dollars giving Esau a total of 24,000 dollars. As his saddlebags were beginning to get somewhat bulky, he asked if there was a way he could have the money transferred to a bank in Missouri.

"Sure, Mister Jones, we can wire transfer it to any bank where you have an account."

Esau wondered why the hell he hadn't already done this instead of packing all that money around with him. He got out his deposit slip from the bank in Independence and handed it to the manager. He then took out two sizeable bundles of one thousand dollar bills amounting to ninety-eight thousand dollars. He left eight one thousand dollar bills in the saddlebag.

"Can you add this ninety-eight thousand to the wire?" asked Esau.

"Yes Sir, I sure can. That will bring your transfer up to $122,000."

"Wait a minute," Esau said as he went back into the saddlebag for more money. Here's six more, make it $128,000.

"Yes Sir, I'll be delighted to."

During this entire transaction Captain Battle watched, awe-stricken.

The $128,000. added to Esau's original twenty-four, brought his account in Independence up to $152,000.

As they started to leave, Esau turned back to the bank manager as he took out two more 1,000 dollar bills. "Sir, could you please change these to 100 dollar bills."

"Certainly Mister Jones, I'll be happy to." They watched him count out twenty 100 dollar bills.

"Thank you, Sir."

Before leaving, when Esau went to the livery to get the Bay, he gave ten 100 dollar bills to Arthur for his help and asked him to take the four carbines from behind the hay down to Captain Battle.

Arthur couldn't stop thanking Esau for the money.

"What're you gon'na do with it, Arthur?"

"Well Sir, sumthin I have dreamed about for some time. I'm gon'na buy that little lot on younder side (he motioned) of the livery, and build me a blacksmith shop, where I can shoe horses. I can stay busy there and still run the livery too. We need a blacksmith shop on this side of town, and now by golly we will have one."

"You think you can do all of that with one thousand dollars?"

"Yes Sir, I believe so. I can get the lot for five hundred, it's just a small lot, but it's all I need. Then I can have a shed built for two or three hundred, and buy the equipment, like an anvil, hammers and horseshoes and such. Yes Sir, if I skimp somewhat, I'll make it, Sir."

Esau reached into his saddlebag and gave Arthur another six hundred dollars. He liked Arthur and was impressed with his desirous proclivity to better his stature.

Chapter 13

The trip from Austin to San Antonio was only about three hours according to Esau's judgment of time. The handlers took four horses off, including the Bay and put them into a corral at the end of the station. There were two horses left on the train for the continuation to Corpus Christi. Passengers going to Laredo got off the train and had a two hour wait in the station for the train coming from Houston and on to Laredo. Esau spent most of the two hours in the corral talking to the Bay. He was outside when the train was loading to be sure the Bay got loaded okay. Esau decided to spend the rest of the trip, leaned back against his saddlebags daydreaming of Maria.

He remembered seeing the innocence of a little girl in her black shinning eyes, as he sit astraddle her in the sand. He remembered the intense pleasure of her breast grinding into his back as she rode behind him on the Bay. He still can't help but believe that some of it was purposely exaggerated, much to his gratification. And at the last meeting in the canyon near the ranch, he time and again, dwelled on what she had said. *I will always love you in my heart.* And then at the meeting in the convent when she couldn't stop kissing him. He was mentally being enveloped with loving kisses by his beautiful nun when he was suddenly thrown forward by a terrific jerking and lurching of the train as it was slowing to a quick stop with the brakes screeching and the wheels screaming.

As the train stopped, Esau thought first, above everything, about the Bay. He picked himself up, grabbed his saddlebag and made it, through the almost hysterical people, to the end door and across to the next car which was the horse car. The two very nervous horses had gotten up, and were along with Esau, thrown again to the floor from a forward swaying lurch which came in unison with a horrific resonating boom.

He tied the unknown horse to a stall side, opened the sliding door, threw his saddlebag over the saddle-horn, tightened the chinch and mounted the Bay. He then carefully jumped him out onto the ground. The Bay went down to his front knees, but righted himself immediately as Esau saw that he was only four cars up from the baggage car with four men on horseback and two horses without riders gathered at the open baggage car. Two more horsemen passed him by at a fast gait coming from the engine. They reined-up by the other horsemen and looked back at Esau. The two men and the other four turned toward Esau as they drew their pistols. Esau, remembering the shooting of the Wild Bunch, as one of these men fired the first shot, he rolled from the Bay telling him to "Git" as he threw his saddlebag to the ground and was firing both pistols accurately before he touched the ground. The Bay ran away from the shooting, as Esau rolled back and forth on the ground dropping the shooters like kingpins. The way the shooters moved around when their horses reared made him think he may have missed some of his shots. As he rolled over on his saddlebag he quickly, without losing focus reached inside it and come out with another six-shooter alike to his others and shot the last two from their saddles, but not before he felt the sting of a bullet.

Esau rolled one final time as the other two men jumped down from the open door and started walking toward him with their guns blazing. Esau noticed that one of them wore a Union Captains Hat. He sat up and pumped numerous shots into their chests. Esau got up and walked over to the final two. He looked down at the man who wore the Union hat and put three more shots into his heart and one in his head.

As a crowd of passengers gathered around from the train, a lady noticed the blood on the left side of Esau's chest. She and a gentleman tore back his shirt to see about the wound. It was a through and through wound to his shoulder. The lady ripped up her petticoat and dressed both sides of the wound.

"That should do it until you see a doctor." said the Lady.

"Thank you mam."

"No, it's you we should all thank, Mister Jones."

"How did you know who I am?"

"Everybody on the train was talking about you. They all said we had nothing to worry about with Esau Jones on the train."

A man said he could run the train and get us on into Laredo. "It's only about thirty miles from here."

A bunch of men pitched in and laid all eight dead men into the baggage car where the safe had been blown open. They pulled out a portable ramp and put the Bay back in the horse car with Esau's help. They had killed the baggage car attendant and the fireman and engineer in the locomotive.

When the train limped into Laredo, someone summoned Marshal Phillip Hancock and told him that Esau Jones had killed the Nathan Montgomery gang.

Marshal Hancock, while Esau went to the doctor, had his two deputies and some helpful spectators to take the three railroad employees and the outlaws to the morgue. He took possession of all of their firearms.

The doctor said it had to be a ball to go completely through as it did. He redressed Esau's wound, gave him a sedative and went with him to be sure he registered at the hotel and told him to go to bed and get a good night's sleep. Esau did just that, falling asleep immediately after getting into bed.

The next morning he went to the Marshals office to see about his bounty money. He had only to sign the Marshal's book for 17 thousand dollars. The Marshal told him that the Bank president had cleared it to pay him an additional 17 thousand from his bank. Esau went to the bank and had the 34 thousand wired to his account at the Independence Bank in Independence, Missouri. This brought his total account up to $186,000.

Bearing the brunt of the intense pain in his left shoulder, he and the Bay took the next train back to San Antonio where they changed trains to the sunset route through south Texas to El Paso. Through the whole trip he thought only of Maria, and how close he had come to biting the dust. That shot could have been through his heart instead of his shoulder. The thought bothered him immensely to think how it would affect Maria if he got himself killed. His foremost thought now was to get back to Missouri and find a place for them to live. He figured the brunt of the winter should be about gone.

"It was nearing noon when the train unloaded in El Paso, Esau rode the Bay to U. S. Marshal Tom Greenstreet's office. Tom looked up from some papers on his desk.

"Hot damn, Esau Jones, did'ya bring me some outlaws?" he stood up and reached across his desk to shake hands. "I'm sure pleased to see you. I heard you got shot."

"Yeah, about four or five days ago. How have you and your boys been?"

"We've been doing just fine. Things have been real slow here. You pretty well cleaned up south Texas, I hear, and I'm pleased to know that mine and Sam's suspicions about Captain Battle were unfounded."

"Yeah, he's an alright Marshal. Have you had dinner yet?"

"I was wondering when you was gon'na ask."

Tom came from around his desk and they went out the door. Tom locked the door.

"Where are your boys?"

"They and Sam Pickett's two deputies from Las Cruces, joined up with three deputies from Fort Stockton with orders from Captain Battle in Austin, to set a trap for Luther Armstrong and his gang, in Presido. They want to catch him coming into the United States from Ojinaga, Mexico. It came from the Captain that he had it from a good source that the Armstrong gang was using that crossing to come in and pull robberies. I hope the restaurant has something good to eat, I'm famished."

"Yeah, me too."

"How many men are in the gang?"

"I believe Armstrong has six men. They are all murderous cut-throats too. They robbed a small bank up in Alpine and killed all three people working in it, for a measly four thousand dollars. They were identified by outside spectators."

Supper had not cooked enough to get into it, so they both settled for warmed over biscuits and fried eggs and naturally two or three cups of hot coffee. Esau told Tom of his plans to stop bounty hunting and go into the horse business. Also, he told about his nun out in California that he planned on taking to Missouri as his bride.

Tom was too flabbergasted to say anything. They finished eating in silence and Esau told him that he was going to ride down to the bridge to see some friends in Mexico. When they returned to the office Esau mounted the Bay and headed to the bridge. He rode the Bay across the bridge and dismounted by the guards.

The Federally border guards were ecstatic to see him. They gathered around him all talking at once. The soldier Capitan that spoke some broken English interjected.

"Senor Esau, Amigo, how you are?" He joined with the others in patting him on the shoulder and lavishing him with salutations.

"Do you wish to capture more Americano banditos."

"Do you have some more staying over here?"

"Si, Senor, we have more." He held up seven fingers. "Si Senor Esau, we have this many right where the others were. You wish, we arrest and tie them in the saddles, like before. We now have made for us, many rawhide leashes." The Capitan had the complete attention of his other comrades, who showed their agreement with many repeated Si's. "We pull off the boots and tie the feet in the stirrups, Si, like before, Si?"

"Si," said Esau. "Like before."

"Pistoles in feed sack. Si? Boots in feed sack, Si?"

"Si, Amigo."

The Capitan said something to the soldiers, indistinguishable to Esau, and they shouldered their rifles and headed down the road through the Mexican village. Esau started to go but the Capitan told him no.

"We let the soldiers do the work. They know what to do."

"Do you know what the head man is called?"

"Si, Senor Esau. He is called Lutter."

"Lutter huh, That must be Luther."

"Si Senor, Lutter."

While they waited at the bridge, Esau dug down under the paraphernalia in one side of his saddlebag and came up with a dozen fifty dollar gold pieces that he had taken as part of the payment on a bounty draft. They waited what seemed to be about two hours before they saw the caravan of cursing and grumbling outlaws being led to the bridge by the Capitan's happy soldiers. The outlaws were bootless and had no hats. Luther Armstrong had on burnt orange long-johns. The soldiers said he was in bed with a women and they couldn't get his clothes on him. They said two others were asleep and the other four were well on their way to becoming drunk in the saloon. One feed sack filled with pistols and holster rigs were tied to one of the horses. Another sack of boots and hats, the soldiers kept as before. Esau gave each of them two fifty dollar gold pieces. He mounted the Bay, and took the reins of the lead horse as the soldiers paid homage to their hero.

Esau paraded the captured outlaws through town back to the Marshall's office. Tom Greenstreet stood on the walk shaking his head as Esau stopped the caravan of outlaws in front of the office. Tom called to a bystander.

"Charlie, will you run over and tell the Sheriff that I need him and his deputies right now."

Esau had dismounted and stepped up on the walk by Tom.

"You can wire Captain Battle and tell him to call off his hunt for Luther Armstrong and his gang."

"You just couldn't stand me taking a rest, could you?"

"At least I didn't kill any of'em."

"By jimmies, that's right—you did good Esau. I will just never understand how the hell you do it,—barefoot and half naked.—Good Lord."

The Sheriff and two deputies showed up in record time.

"With this many, I spoze we ought to shackle'em in the prisoner transfer car out yonder on the sidetrack. The train will be here in four days to take'em to Bastrop," said Tom.

"Alright Tom," answered the Sheriff. "I'll hire on two more deputies so's to have enough to watch'em and feed'em."

Esau removed the sack of firearms and rigs from the last horse and the Sheriff with his two deputies lead them away toward the railroad, to the prisoner transfer car, where they were all shackled into their seats to await the west bound train. Esau and Tom went into the Marshal's office. Tom went through his posters and found the Luther Armstrong gang. It listed his gang individually by name with a one thousand bounty on each of them and a ten thousand dollar bounty on Luther, all listed as dead or alive. Tom made out the government draft to Esau Jones, bounty hunter, in the amount of $16,000.

Before going to the bank, Esau and Tom chatted awhile with Esau telling him he intended to catch the train day after tomorrow that goes up through Tucumcari and on to Kansas City.

"I've heard tell, it's nigh on close enough to springtime, that the track should be open." Esau said, as he looked at Tom for his reaction.

"Yeah, it's just around the corner—could be, it'll come early this year.—It's

bout supper time."

"I'll go to the bank and meet'ya over to the restaurant."

"Okay."

At the bank Esau had fifteen thousand of the bounty draft wired to Independence and kept one thousand in one hundred dollar bills. The wire brought the account in Independence, as best Esau had figured, up to $201,000.

Supper went down pretty good, with smothered liver and onions and lumpy mashed potatoes. Esau actually enjoyed it, not every having smothered liver as he could remember since he was a young lad on the farm.

"What will you be doing tomorrow," asked Tom.

"Don't rightly know, cept for one thing. I'm go'na send a love telegram to my nun, out in California. I'm gon'na wire sweet endearments to the love of my life."

"I've got to go," said Tom as he arose. "I feel like I'm getting sick."

"Must be the liver," said Esau.

149

Esau did indeed send a telegram to Maria, telling her he loved her dearly and that he was on his way back from Texas to Missouri. He told her he was quitting the bounty hunting and was going back to find a place for the horse farm, now that he could afford it. He said that he would be sending for her and Jose and Rosa before the end of spring. He ended with another endearment of love, and gave the telegrapher an extra twenty dollars to send for delivery to the San Miguel Mission.

Esau also wired Marshal Sam Logan in Santa Fe and ask him to share the wire with Bill Carson. He told them of his immediate plans, and said that he would surely see them once he got settled. He told them he had just wired Maria about his plans for her and Jose and Rosa. *"I hope I have a hoss there to pick up,"* he added.

After sending the second wire he asked the telegrapher what month of the year it was.

"Sir, it is almost the end of April. Spring has sprung. It may still be kind of chilly to the north, but that won't last long."

The next stop was the depot. He bought his ticket to Kansas City for himself and the Bay. His train will leave at ten a.m. and *"Yes"* the agent said. *"The tracks are clear all the way through to St. Louis."*

Esau slept good, ate some breakfast, and was at the depot when the train pulled in. He helped load the Bay, rubbed his nose and talked to him before going to his passenger car with his saddlebag slung across his shoulder and boarding the train to start a completely new life filled with love and admiration beyond his wildest dreams.

Chapter 14

Much to Esau's gratification the train pulled into the station in Kansas City, Missouri. He could hardly wait to get off and stretch his legs. He went right to the horse car and waited for the wranglers to put down the ramp and bring the horses out. He took the Bay off to the side and rubbed and talked to him. A wrangler came over and spoke to him.

"He's a very nice Bay Mister Esau. Don't forget to tighten the chinch."

"Thanks, I'll bet he's ready to get off the train, I know I am."

"I can certainly understand, but I'm use to it. You have a nice day."

"Thanks, you too."

Esau tightened the saddle chinch and headed to Independence. He first went to the post office, but had no mail. He checked with the bank to see if he had any messages, and checked his account. There were no messages and his balance was $202,000. A little more than he had figured.

He left Independence and rode down to Blue Springs where he checked in with Sheriff Matt Murdock.

"Esau Jones, man I'm glad to see you." The Sheriff jumped up and shook his hand. He then pulled up a chair for Esau to sit down. "I haven't heard anything about you, and was beginning to get worried."

"I've been doing okay, mostly been all over south Texas. That's some big country down there. It takes a while to get around it."

"Yeah, I can imagine. Fredrick Bumgartner got back about two weeks ago. I told him all about you. He said he ain't doing nothing until he talks to you. He knows all about your background, we talked about it, and then I found out that he has all of the books they done about you. He seemed to really like them. When do you want to go out there. He's really anxious to see you."

"Well hell, it's only bout mid-day, you won't to go now?"

'Sure, let's go." Esau had hitched the Bay beside the Sheriff's horse, they mounted them and rode down the road to the big beautiful home. Esau was mentally telling himself to not get his hopes up, let the man do the talking. They rode through the gate and up to the front of the big home. It was even bigger up close. Esau's heart was in his throat as they dismounted and tied the mounts to rings on two hitching posts. Esau put his left hand gun in his saddlebag and hung his other rig over his saddle horn. He followed the Sheriff up onto the wide porch. He had never seen such a big door. The Sheriff sounded a clapper on the door. The door opened and a white haired colored man dressed in an elegant butler uniform invited them in.

"Hello Mister Murdock, and yes Sir," he extended his hand with a white linen glove. "You're Mister Jones, I am pleased to meet you." Esau shook his hand and smiled.

"So, George," the Sheriff said. "How have you been. Is Mister Fredrick available?"

"I've been fine, Mister Matt, He's in the study, I'll get him for y'all."

George turned and went through a set of double doors. As Esau admired the interior of the entranceway, Mister Bumgartner came in and greeted them like old friends as he had them to follow him into the study. He seated them in comfortable chairs and rang a little hand bell, which a uniformed colored servant girl responded to in quick order. He asked what they would like to drink. Esau spoke up first with a request for black coffee. Fredrick smiled and followed suit as did the Sheriff.

"Well, Esau Jones." Bumgartner said intriguingly as he stroked his chin. "I feel as if I know you very personally. I know of your young days when you rode as a renegade bushwhacker with Captain William Quantrill and Captain William Anderson, not to mention your days with Captain Archie Clements."

The servant came in pushing a cart with a coffee pot and cups on it. She served each man individually, pouring his coffee with a pleasing bow. She pushed the cart to the side and bowed out graciously.

"All of the help here are sometime more gracious than expected to be. That either comes from loving their jobs or gratification for allowing them to stay after Lincoln's Emancipation Proclamation was signed into law on January first, eighteen sixty-three. Not any of my people on the farm wanted to be emancipated. We had thirteen slaves that worked and lived here on the farm like a big happy family. We knew each one personally and saw to their needs. Even two years after Elizabeth's demise, I still have all thirteen.

There is George, the butler, Birdie, the cook, You will like Birdie, but just don't go into her kitchen messing around. Then there is Denise, she was Elizabeth's dresser. Ruth, Emily and Rose are waitresses, and Viola, Mercie and Etta are chambermaids. They all pitch in with the house cleaning. They help each other out when need be and work good together. Then there is Jobe and his wife Elena, and two strapping sons, Roy and Bud. They live in the second house over to the left in what is referred to as the section. The men over there have stables beside each individual house where they keep their personal steeds. Jobe is one of the most proficient cowboys in working with horses that you will find. Roy and Bud are learning all of the secrets from him. We also have a Mexican family in the third house over in the section. I had heard that Carlos worked at the horse corrals in Forth Worth. He had a reputation of having an inner sensibility in the training of good horses. He worked with wild horses shipped in from the northeast grass plains of Wyoming. There are a lot of good stock out there, especially brood mares. They are much better than the wild Mustangs out of Nevada and Utah. Anyway, Carlos Cadero, agreed to come and work on our farm. His wife, Lupe, was expecting and he needed to settle her down in a comfortable home. They have loved it here and we all love them. Little Pedro, their son recently turned twelve. Time has sure flown by.

"I tell you this about Carlos and his family, because I know of your Spanish bride to be and her Godparents. And just in case we work something out in the future, I wanted to let you know that, there is a small Catholic Church in Blue Springs where Carlos and his family goes." "Would ya'll like your coffee warmed. I'll call Ruth back in."

Esau was first to speak. "Yeah, that would be nice."

Fredrick rang his bell and the girl came right in. Fredrick just motioned to the coffee cart and she went right out with it.

"Yes Esau, I know you well. I knew of your ordeal of being in Tennessee when the redleg militia killed your parents and sister before burning the farm. I have known of your apathy for the redlegs every since. I have learned of your bounty hunting escapades to raise money to start a horse farm and have a place to house your beloved. And I must say that you have done a marvelous job.

Ruth rolled the cart in and again poured all three men a hot cup of coffee. She then took her leave, turning and curtsying before going out the door.

"Now Esau, you understand that I know about you, and I truly believe that destiny has brought us together. You're looking for a horse farm, and I'm wanting to get out from under one. So now it's time to tell you about me. Let's drink our coffee and go walk around outside. First of all, I left off to quick on the farms populous. There are two more families of working hands and two single men, Jim Conners, who is acting as caretaker. He is also a very good hand at training working horses. In all, excluding the kids, the populace of the farm still totals twenty-two good, honest and righteous people. They are all good hands that know and excel in their jobs. The other single man is the Forman. What say we go for a walk."

Outside, Fredrick had to stop and admire the Bay, patting his neck and giving him compliments. *"He sure nuff does know his hoss flesh."* thought Esau. He asked Esau how long he had ridden him. Esau told him, showing him the musket ball wounds the Bay had received.

"Good Lord, Esau, it's time you retired him to stud."

"Yeah, I know, That's my intention."

"You boys have fun," the Sheriff said. "I have to go make a living. It's been a good visit Fred, I'll see you later. You too Esau." Sheriff Murdock mounted his steed and rode away.

"Esau, why don't you bring the Bay and put him in a corral out back. You can unsaddle him and let him water and eat. Put your saddle and gear inside the stable least it comes a rain. I don't look for rain today but you never know. Esau led the Bay around to the back of the big home and across about fifty yards of groomed lawn, crossing a wagon road that completely encircled the house. He admired the barn, stables and various corrals and holding pens. Esau unsaddled the Bay and put him in a corral next to one that the Appaloosa geldings were in. He took the bridle off and the Bay went right to the corral water tank. Esau noticed that each corral had a water tank and a feed trough. The water tanks were fed by a single windmill pump piped to each tank

"Mister Bumgartner Sir, —

"Esau, Please just call me Fred, it's much easier and friendly."

"Yes Sir, I was going to say what beautiful Appaloosa geldings they are." He motioned to the geldings.

"Oh yes, that's Pete and Repeat, they were the love of Kitty's life."

Esau looked questioningly at Fredrick.

"Oh, I'm sorry, Kitty was my pet name for my wife Elizabeth. I called her that most of the time."

"Yes, that is a nice name, I bet she liked it."

"Yes, she did, she —she—

Esau immediately noticed his grief caused by the recollection of his wife.

"Fred, what breed of horse did you have the best luck with?"

The two men walked as they talked.

"We had quite a few different breeds. You could never tell what possessed a person to pick a certain breed for his personal saddle horse. Now cattle ranches that want the best in working cow horses for fast reining and cutting were different. They would usually choose smaller horses, about fourteen or fifteen hands high and strong well muscled body, yet agile. They would be mainly in the family of the Chestnut, Choctaw, Brown, Buckskin, and Duns. Now good saddle horses come in all colors, the most favored seem to be the Bays, Roans, and Sorrels, showing the true red brown colors with splashes of yellow on the Sorrels. Roans are more prominently red than are the Bays, except naturally the Blue Roan. These saddle horses for the discriminating horseman are well muscled and stand sixteen to seventeen hands. Also the solid black or solid white Arabian are popular saddle horses. My favorite is the white Arabian with black main and tail. We sold a number of them. Then for the lady equestrian we had the smaller Paints and Palominos. A favorite for the ladies was one that I crossbred between a dark brown Chestnut stud and a white Arabian mare. It produced a most beautiful brown and white show-horse, similar to a red and white Paint. We acquired eight more white Arabian mares and produced eight more such colts each year. They were all sold in advance of training them as two year olds, for I might add, a top price of sixteen hundred each." They had walked through the stables, came back around through the barn where Esau noticed many sacks of unused oats and a loft full of hay bales, Parked under a shed on the back side of the barn he saw a most luxurious four seat carriage with a fringed top. On the east side of the barn was a bunkhouse running the whole length of the barn. It housed the unmarried farm hands that worked from time to time during horse breaking time.

As they walked back near the Bay, Fredrick saw Jobe Washington's boys, Roy and Bud over near the section and whistled. He then motioned for them to come over. "That's another fine family that's been with us since the beginning."

The two strapping teen-age colored boys came running up.

"Roy,—Bud, how have you been?"

"Good Sir," they said together.

"This is Mister Jones boys. How about giving his Bay some oats and rub him down."

"Yes Sir," said Roy. "We will take good care of him for'ya Mister Jones."

"Oh Bud, Mister Jones laid his saddle and gear in the stable. Will you get his saddle off of the ground, and then take his saddlebags and guns into George and tell him to put them in a guest room."

"Yes Sir, Mister Fred, I'll do it right now."

Esau and Fred walked out across the field toward a distant stand of cottonwood trees in bloom growing in a low area containing a bubbling spring.

"Now, about me Esau. Back during the war, I did something that I am until this day, still ashamed of. I allowed a Union General to commandeer my home for use as his command post on their push south. I told my loving wife to play along as a Union sympathizer. Otherwise we would have been killed and our home burned. We played the part as Unionist to the hilt, knowing full well we hated them with a gnawing passion.

I however did take risky chances, going horseback below the line into Confederate field hospitals to deliver much needed Quinine. Had I been caught I would have been killed on the spot."

"Where did you get the quinine?"

"A doctor that was a good friend in Kansas City furnished me with bags of it. I think he got it from virtually every doctor in Kansas City, or possibly from the medicinal wholesale house."

"You were taking a hell'of'a chance doing that, but you probably saved many a'life. I remember myself how hard Quinine was to come by."

"Now Esau, the reason I am telling you all of this is because before we make any kind of deal on the farm, I want you to know me, and I want to be assured that the people living here will remain with a well meaning owner."

"Yes, I understand."

"Kitty and I, in our young years, had a live energetic ambition for excitement. We were of the pioneering spirit and decided to leave England for the New World, and build us a life here. At that time it was the talk of England how this young country was growing and building. So we caught a ship and landed in New York with droves of other adventurous pioneers. After traveling by covered wagon about a year we wound up staying for a while near Baton Rouge. After a while we headed back north, and after looking over the countryside and the local people we decided on taking roots here in Blue Springs. We both wanted to raise thoroughbred horses, a thing that we held in great interest from England. So I had the home built for her to her specifications. We brought our first horses in to the farm in the summer of 1847. Everything went great for about fifteen years. We were ecstatically happy. Young colts kicking up their heels and running across these hills are truly a sight to see. Most of the people working here have been with us since the first days. Two of the waitress girls and two of the chambermaids joined us about six years ago. They were relatives of Birdies. True, we had bought some young hardy slaves, but they were never looked on as slaves, but more as members of the family of the Bumgartner Horse Farm. There use to be a sign over the big front gate, but I had it removed when the horses were gone."

"What happened to your horses?"

"The Union Army confiscated them for their cavalry."

"Damn, riding mounts like yours is probably the edge they needed to win the war." They both laughed.

"The General made them leave Elizabeth's gelding buggy horses, and didn't bother the farm hands personal mounts. He had been led to believe that the hands were all pro-Union. They played their roles to perfection. Some days you could hear them over in the section singing Union hymns.—About the horses, brings something else to mind that you need to know. You have not yet met your Foreman, August Mann, He is the other single man that lives in the bunkhouse. Auggy, he is called, is worth any ten men. He is right now in Wyoming rounding up and breaking wild horses with cowboys he hired there. Sometime this summer he will come in here with forty-five horses for the farm, probably all brood mares. I say forty-five because they will be shipped in by train and they can only put fifteen stalls to the car. His plans were to use four horse cars. One would be for cowboys horses. They have to come here with Auggy to help him bring them to the farm from Kansas City. He will then send them back. They halter the horses and blindfold them tied in a stall for shipment."

"Damn," said Esau.

"Yeah, I know, but it keeps them settled down.—When Lincoln was elected to the presidency on the Emancipation platform, I knew then that a war was coming. It just never dawned on me that it would reach us here in Missouri. Anyway, I didn't try to stock the farm back up, because my darling Kitty had taken ill with that damn consumption. I had every doctor in the area trying to help her. They said to just keep her comfortable. Toward the end she was almost living on opium to ease the pain. So Esau, here we are, I have twenty people that I love and need to care for, yet I cannot bring myself to live here without my wife—my love."

"Fred, if we can possibly work out a way for me to buy the farm, I assure you it will be run as you would want, with all of your people, in the memory of your Kitty, and you. I was told that you wished to return to England. What will you do there?"

"Esau, I have a flat there, but I spend my time in a gentleman's private club, where I read, doze and play bridge with gentlemen friends. There is no need to worry about me. I am well healed financially."

"Fred, if we do come to the understanding which I mentioned. I will have to insist on ownership and not a working arrangement. I must be allowed the initiative to operate the farm on my own sense of abilities, not withstanding what I have already deemed necessary about keeping your capable staff."

Fredrick Bumgartner looked into Esau's eyes with resounding pleasure as a knowing smile crossed his face.

"Esau, I was an ardent admirer of Quantrill and Anderson, and the people who rode with them, and knowing that you were one of them serving the cause of the Confederacy, makes me very proud of you. If ever I had been blessed with a son I would have been pleased that he should be like you."

"Are you trying to make me cry—thank you Fred, I appreciate the compliment. Listen, did you ever know the Younger family, Cole, Jim and the others. They were born and raised only about ten miles east of here, about five miles from where my Paw's farm was."

"Yes, I know, but no, I never met them. I have always wished I had. What say, let's you and I ride into Blue Springs in the morning after Birdie feeds us, and go have the banker draw up a quick deed purchase agreement. I want to be getting on back to England. Right now let's go in and let them know you're spending the night so we can get some supper. Now Esau, don't fret about the price, I'll take it easy on you. I know how much money you have in the Independence bank and I know you have to support your farm for at least two and a half years before you begin to turn a profit on your first horses. The horses that Auggy will be bringing in will be a good start, but you will still have to locate some good bred studs. When I sent him after the wild horses, I had in mind, against my wishes, of running the farm some more on account of the fine people living here. And then you came along. Praise the Good Lord.—I'll have Jim Conners hitch up the carriage in the morning and we'll take it.—Oh, by the way, Auggy does not have a family, except for the people here, and he stays in the bunk house with Jim. All of the cowboys that help bring the horses in will probably stay for a few days before returning to Wyoming. Auggy took money with him for expenses, like wages and rental for horse cars and train passage. If he has any left he will give it to you, if he didn't have enough he will tell you. Auggy is one of the most trustworthy men who will ever know."

"When my people get here, I will have Jose Sanchez, take the job as my comptroller. He is a very smart man, he ran the business as comptroller for his brother and Maria's late husband on the Double-Bar-M Ranch."

Fredrick looked pleased that Esau was putting the business end all together in his head. He smiled at him. "You've about got it all ready to start training horses."

Chapter 15

After ham and eggs with grits and red-eye gravy mopped up with hot biscuits, Esau was in love with a two hundred fifty pound roly-poly Birdie. Last evening at supper he had not met her. They were waited on in the dining room by one of the waitress staff. The following morning they had breakfast in another dining room in the back of the house where Birdie would feed the men from the bunkhouse when they had a bunch of bronco breakers working. Esau saw the bunkhouse out on the side of the barn and also discovered that the entire house staff had rooms on the ground floor in the back on the west side. The more Esau found out about how the house was structured for the benefit of the staff to make it run to its greatest effectiveness, the more amazed he became.

Jim Conners, the only hand staying in the bunkhouse, had eaten earlier and had the Appaloosa gelding's hitched to the carriage and waiting out back.

"Well, what say we get started," said Fredrick as he got up from the table.

"Let me go to my room for just a second."

Esau went up to the guest room, made sure his pistol was fully loaded and put it in his waistband under his shirt.

"I'm ready to go, Fred."

They went out the back screen door to where Jim Conners waited at the carriage.

"Do you want me to drive y'all," asked Jim.

"No thanks Jim, we'll do fine.—Oh, Jim, when we return, I have an announcement to make to the entire staff. Will you let them know, so they will be prepared and not out of hand someplace."

"Yes Sir, I'll tell them. Y'all have a nice drive."

Fredrick took the reins, clicked at the horses, and with their heads held high, the geldings set and maintained a smooth pace around the house and down through the front gate. After turning to the right and high stepping for about a mile, Fredrick pulled them over and stopped on the bluff road above a beautiful spring feed lake about a mile wide and three miles long. The lake for which the town of Blue Springs was named.

"I have always liked to stop and admire the lake." Fredrick said. "It puts a feeling of serenity in my soul that kind of lights up my day."

"It is certainly a beautiful sight. I have stopped too, and looked at it every time I come this way."

"I noticed Esau, that you brought a pistol with you."

"I had to Fredrick, I'm always leery that some wandering redleg will want to kill me. I long for the day when I no longer will have to carry protection. The day when I'm no longer looked at as a bounty hunter or an enemy of anyone."

"Yes, I remember the time when I carried that same fear, only for different reasons,—by the way Esau, in the closet of your master bedroom, you will find a box which contains a matched set of old Army ball and cap colts, and underarm holster straps. There are some suits with loose coats for the purpose of concealing them. We are of the same statue, so I'm sure they will fit you. I'm not going to be taking anything with me but a small valise. The train leaves for New York early in the morning that I want to take because it will get me there in time to connect with a steamer for England. The next ship will be in another two months. So, I'm leaving you with everything. You will find all the operating books in the desk, in the study. I'll be saying all of my good-bye's tonight.

When the carriage pulled up in front of the Blue Springs Bank, Fredrick got out and tied the horses to a rail. Esau met him on the walk and they went into the Bank. Esau was unaware what was going to transpire in the Bank.

Upon going into the bank, Fredrick introduced Esau to the President, Able James.

"Able has always done my legal work for me. He's better informed in law than any lawyer I've ever met." Esau smiled and shook Able James's hand while wondering if he may be related to Frank and Jesse. He started to ask him, but thought better of it.

"Alright Able, here's what I want.—Draw up me a quick sale deed for the 360 acre property on Lakeshore Drive know as the Fredrick Bumgartner Horse Farm. Put me down as seller and put Esau Jones down as buyer."

"You finally found you a buyer, Fred."

"Yeah, I sure did.—Make it to read thusly, I, Fredrick Bumgartner, do hereby sale the aforementioned property to Esau Jones for the total price of One Hundred dollars, and other valuable considerations. Make a line for me to sign it and put his name on it as buyer.—When you get it drawn up and we sign it, you can witness it and take it over to the Land Office at the Courthouse and register it.—To make this legal, Esau, you have to give me a hundred dollars in Able's presence."

Esau couldn't wipe the doltish grin off his face as he took the hundred dollars from his pocket and handed it to Fredrick.

After the signing had been accomplished, Fredrick and Esau got in the carriage and Fredrick high-stepped the beautiful Appaloosa's the thirty odd miles to the Kansas City train depot. Fredrick purchased his ticket to New York and they found a restaurant where they had dinner and talked horses for an hour before heading back to the Farm.

The carriage pulled up near the Archway and stopped.

"Esau, You have a nice home to bring your bride to. I think the old sign is in the barn. You'll have to get it scrapped and cleaned, and have your name painted on it, Esau Jones, Horse Farm."

"No, I think I'll just call it, Jones Horse Farm."

"Sure, that sounds good. Let's get on up to the house and get some coffee. I have to be back to the depot by ten o'clock in the morning. I'm really dreading these good-byes. Saying good-bye is such a despairing thing to do, there is no way to alleviate the unhappiness."

Fredrick pulled the carriage around to the back. Jim came out and held the horses as they got out.

"I'll unhitch'em and rub'em down."

"I'll need them harnessed back up in the morning in time to leave again by eight o'clock in the morning."

"Yes Sir."

"In the morning you can go with us."

Jim perked up. "Yes Sir."

After Fredrick said good-bye to all the household servants, gathered in the large dining room, and hugged each of them. He introduced them to the new owner, Esau Jones, and assured them that their position would remain the same. He then, along with Esau, went to the section and did the same with everyone living there. Esau got to meet all of them. He asked Carlos and his wife how they got to church. Carlos showed him a wagon out behind his house and told him his horse pulled it. Esau told him about Maria, Jose and Rosa, and told him from now on they will take the carriage with them, that is, after they get here. Carlos and Lupe expressed their graciousness.

When morning came, Birdie sent them all off with a good hot breakfast in the back dining room.

"Jim," Fred asked. "How long do you suppose it will be before Auggy gets here with the new mares?"

Jim thought for a moment and was figuring on his fingers. "Well, I reckon it should be, beings how they was going to corral them in a box canyon to break'em, it should ought'ta be another five or six weeks. It will take a while for ten men to break forty-five hosses, good enough to halter lead'em."

Fred took a sip of coffee and answered. "Jim, when he gets here you tell him of the ownership change and introduce him to Esau." He had hoped Auggy would be back before he left. But it just wasn't to be. *"Perhap's he would write to him later, from England."*

"Yes Sir, I'll let him know first thing. I can't wait ta'see all them new hosses."

Esau was taking it all in while he enjoyed his breakfast and hot coffee.

They got away at eight o'clock with Jim driving and arrived at the Kansas City Depot at nine-thirty. Fredrick hugged both of them and gave Esau an extra squeeze for reassurance and told him to, as if talking to a son, conduct himself with the dignity of a respected horse farm owner and breeder. He boarded the train and they waited until it pulled out before heading home,

The rest of the day Esau better explored the surroundings. He saw the six foot high fence running straight back from the back corner of the bunkhouse and disappearing into the woods. From the same corner of the bunkhouse, another high fence ran directly east to the far end of the property. Esau deduced that the fenced in acreage was for holding the stallions. He had missed it before because of going through the barn instead of around the bunkhouse. He then went into the house and moved into the master bedroom. After dinner he told George and Birdie that he would be going the next morning to send some telegrams to Maria and her Godparents about making plans to come home. He confided all of his plans and life to them. He told Jim about the sorrel he had in Santa Fe, and that he may have to go there himself to bring him to the farm. He wasn't sure yet, he may have someone to bring him. He was thinking of Carl, but wasn't sure of anything. He told Jim, that come morning to saddle the Bay for him to go into town on.

During the night Esau shaved and cleaned up. He tried on one of the dark pen-striped suits that Fred left him. It fit perfectly, and hid the underarm holsters and six-guns. He checked out the ball and cap forty-fives for weight and balance. He then cleaned them, loaded them, holstered them and took the rig off. He was very impressed with himself in the big dressing mirror with the suit on. He couldn't relish the derby hats. They just wasn't him. He would buy him a new hat, similar to the one he wore. Maybe black—no, white he thought would be best. He finally went to bed and caught a little sleep.

Morning came early for Esau. He was up and dressed by sun up. He put on a clean white shirt with lace down the front, and found in back of the closet two practically new pairs of black boots, that fit just right. After putting on the pants, he put on the boots and changed his spurs over to them, put on the double gun rig and the coat over it. He thought he could almost be mistaken for Wyatt Earp, from pictures he has seen of him, except for the mustache. *"Why"* he thought. *"Am I standing here admiring myself, like a woman."* The thought gave Esau a feeling of shame. He put on his old beat up hat and went downstairs. George was near the door sitting in an easy chair.

"Good morning, Mister Jones. My, you sure does look elegant this morning."

"Thank you George. Do you think I could get Birdie to give me some coffee?"

"You could just sit at the table and ring the little bell, Sir."

"Naugh George, I'll just go back to the back eating room, Jim will probably be coming in."

"Yes Sir, I'll go with you, if'n it's alright."

"Sure George, come on."

Esau not only had coffee, but Birdie, humming a delightful tune, feed him along with Jim and George."

"Lordy' mercy, Mister Jones, don't you just look downright spiffy this morning."

"Thank you Birdie—I reckon."

Esau and Jim went out to get the Bay. George said to Birdie. "Ya'know, I'm gon'na really like Mister Jones, he don't mind at all about eating with the hired help. Yes'sir'ree, he's a good man."

"I could of telled you that, ya'know he was raised just a little way from here. He's from good people. You can tell by his name, Esau. You know he sold his birthright to his twin brother Jacob."

"Hush yer mouth woman, what you talking bout?"

Jim already had the Bay saddled and Esau was on his way to the telegraph office in Blue Springs.

It seemed to take him no time to go the few miles. It was the first time he had been on the Bay for awhile, and he was spirited, and wanted to run. He went in first to see Sheriff Murdock. The sheriff looked up as Esau entered.

"Yes Sir, can I———. Esau?—What in tarnation happened to you, holy-cow man, you sure do clean up good. You look like a different person."

"How do you like it Matt?"

"You sure do look dapper. Like a regular business man."

"I am a business man Matt, I run a hoss farm. I bought out Fredrick Bumgartner's spread. He's on his way back to England."

"Holy-cow, Esau, you did it, you got the big plantation home. I figured some kind of deal was brewing when I left y'all. I'm really happy fer'ya Esau."

"Matt, do you know the Priest at the Catholic church here?"

"Sure, I know'em, his name is O'Brian, Father Michael O'Brian, a good friendly man. I talk to'em on occasion. Why?"

"Well, I thought I may get him to write a telegram to the Mother Superior where Maria is to assure her of the legitimacy of my occupation as a hoss farmer. And he also should know there will be three new members in his congregation along with Carlos and his wife."

"I tell you what Esau, I'll take you to see him, he lives right behind his church."

"Right now?"

"Yeah, let's go, he'll be glad to see us."

Esau removed his coat, took his twin gun rig off, and hung it on Matt's coat rack.

"Man, that's sure an admirable set of old Army Colt's, pearl handle and all, man Esau, you're really something else."

The Church being only three blocks from the Sheriff's office, Matt and Esau walked to it, and Matt knocked on the door of the rear house. Father O'Brian answered the door and bid them in. Esau related the whole story to the Father, including his reasoning as to Mother Angelina needing more proof than just his word.

"I will most certainly send her the telegram on your behalf, Mister Jones. It will be my pleasure, I have been worried about the disposition of the plantation, for the sake of Carlos, and also for the other folks out there. I was very happy to hear of it having a new owner and everyone was staying. Now, Mister Jones, if you don't go to California to get them, and they come in to Kansas City on the train, I would be more than grateful to perform the wedding. I'm sure your Maria would like to have a Catholic wedding."

"By all means Father, I will certainly look forward to it, and thank you very much. Oh, let me give you the address of the mission in San Miguel. He reached into his inside pocket and pulled out some papers with all of his names and addresses on it. Father O'Brian wrote down the address Esau then handed him three hundred dollars.

"This will cover it Father, with some left for your coffers."

The Priest started to make a protest and Esau stopped him.

"Please Father, it is something I wish to do."

"Thank you, my son, the telegram will be sent this afternoon. Oh, by the way, I normally deliver my sermons in English, all of my congregation speak English, and some of them Italian. Will English be sufficient for your Maria and her Godparents, or should I interpose with Spanish."

"Well, Father, you deliver your sermon however you see fit. Maria, Jose and Rosa speak fluent English, as well as Spanish. Maria was schooled at Columbia University in New York."

"That is absolutely amazing Mister Jones, I can hardly wait to meet them. What languishes do you speak?"

"I speak Missouri brogue and a bit of Cherokee."

Esau graciously thanked him. The Sheriff, and he walked back to the Sheriff's office. He put his gun rig back on and decided to go on up to Kansas City, and check in with Marshall Henry Hancock. He had something he wanted the Marshall to do for him. He also wanted to send Maria a telegram.

The ride on the Bay was the most enjoyable trip he had recently taken. His head was clear of worries about getting a farm and sending for Maria. The air was fresh, the country was beautiful with blooms sprouting on the trees, the birds singing and spring in the air,—KA-BANG, a lone loud rifle shot rang out and echoed through the woods. Esau fell from his horse. A rider came up out of the ravine just behind him. The rider dismounted and approached Esau with rifle in hand, he turned Esau over with a vigorous push of his boot, Esau immediately put two balls through the man's heart, who fell back as Esau rolled from under the man's rifle, although the man didn't have enough life left in him to pull his trigger before falling dead. Esau had a slight burn crease on the side of his head. He did not know the man, so he tied him across his saddle and led him on into Kansas City to Marshall Hancock, and told him what happened. He then went to the barber shop and had the barber to brush him off as best he could, and wash the side of his head. The barber was elated to see him and told him, after rubbing some medicinal ointment into the burn on his head, to come back and get a free shave.

Henry Hancock was still, along with the local mortician, trying to get a fix on the dead man's identity.

"Henry, there was something I came to ask you to do for me. I've bought a horse farm, I'm getting married and retiring from bounty hunting. I would like for you to let the Marshall's across Texas, Arizona and New Mexico know I've retired so they don't think I'm dead, even though I almost just was.—I know what, wire Captain Battle in Austin, he can get the word out.—No, Henry, forget it, I'll wire the Captain, myself."

Marshall Hancock stared at Esau for a long while before speaking, trying to comprehend everything he had said. He thought perhaps his head injury was bothering him.

"Esau, are you feeling alright?"

"Yeah Henry, I'm fine, I'm going to the telegraph office, I'll be back."

"Okay Esau, be sure you come back."

Chapter 16

Esau wired the U.S Marshall's office in Austin and told Captain Battle to let all of his friends know that he was retired. He then wired Maria and told her that he had a home for her, Jose and Rosa. He assured her that she would like it, and pledged his undying love for her. He told her of the local Priest that was going to marry them. *"And tell Jose, we will be raising thoroughbred hosses, and I would like it, if he is willing, for him to be the business manager, or comptroller, as he was at the Double-Bar-M. We will have about twenty-five people working on the farm. The Priest is wiring Mother Angelina with the conformation of our hoss ranch, and my retiring from bounty hunting. I am wiring money to Jose at the Bank of Paso Robles for travel expenses. Ya'll can take the train from there all the way through to Kansas City. Tell Jose to wire the Sheriff, Matt Murdock, in Blue Springs, Missouri with y'alls arrival date in Kansas City, and someone will be there to pick you up. Our bank account is at the Independence Bank in both our names in case you need more money. Independence is forty miles from Kansas City. Our home is another few miles just outside of Blue Springs. All my love, Esau."*

This wire is go'na cost you a small fortune, Mister Jones."

"Add twenty dollars to it for delivery to the mission."

"Yes Sir."

When Esau returned to Henry's office, they had discovered the identity of his assailant. A deputy found it in the saddlebag of the dead man.

"Do you remember killing a man named Rufus Musgrove down at Blue Springs."

"Yeah, as a matter of fact I do. I had to shoot'em right in front of the hotel. He was one of the four Willy Bunch."

"Well, this fellow is, or was, a brother to the deceased Rufus Musgrove. He more than likely has been looking for you ever since to avenge his brother's death. There ain't no wanted poster on him, he just had a vengeance for retribution."

"He came damn close to collecting it too. My head is still burning where that slug creased it. That's two close calls I've had."

"What was the other one, Esau?"

"I caught a bullet, or I think It might have been a ball, clean through my left shoulder, bout six inches from my heart while discombobulating a train robbery outside of Laredo, Texas."

"You have a dangerous occupation, Esau. Kind'a like riding with the devil, you never know when he will take you."

Esau stared at Henry, trying to figure out exactly what he meant. He let it drop. "Henry, I better go, I need to get to the bank at Independence before it closes."

"Take care, Esau, and keep a close watch behind'ya"

"Yeah, thanks.'

Esau asked the banker at Independence to wire five thousand dollars to be picked up by Jose Sanchez, to the bank of Paso Robles in Paso Robles, California.

He then went on to Blue Springs to talk to Sheriff Murdock. He told him about Rufus Musgrove's brother almost doing him in and told him to expect a wire from Jose Sanchez as to their arrival in Kansas City. "Would you mind riding out to the house when you get the wire?"

"Sure Esau, I'll be glad to do whatever I can."

"I'm going back down to the telegraph office, I'll be back later."

"You sure are sending a powerful lot of telegrams today."

"Yeah, I sure am."

Esau had harbored the idea of going to Santa Fe, but gave it up to try to handle his business by telegraph. He decided that he didn't want to be camped out somewhere between Tucumcari and Santa Fe, going after a hoss he wasn't even sure was there. No, he wanted to be here when Maria arrived. So, he sent another telegram.

To; U.S. Marshall Sam Logan, Santa Fe, New Mexico.

"Hi Sam, wire me back with disposition of the sorrel, share this wire with Bill Carson and Carl from Double-Bar-M, and tell him to contact me through Sheriff, Matt Murdock, Blue Springs, Missouri. I have purchased a hoss farm in Blue Springs, and have sent for Maria, Jose and Rosa. Find out if the livery still has the DBM carriage and team. If so, I would like Carl to buy it, clean it up, and take it to the DBM, crate the two things in the safe room, load them into the carriage, and bring the Pinto back to Santa Fe, pick up the sorrel and saddle, if relevant, and come to

Blue Springs. Get Ed Trusdale to help him. I have good jobs for both. Unless, that is, they have a better thing going. If this can be done, let me know when you wire, and I will send ample money to your bank to handle all cost. Friends always, Esau Jones."

"You sure send long messages, Mister Jones, would you like me to edit it for you. You know we have to charge by the word."

"No, send it as is, please. What is the cost?"

The telegrapher counted the words. "That will be thirty-seven dollars, sir."

Esau gave him forty dollars and went back to the sheriff's office.

"Matt, I should be getting a wire, sent in care of you. I'll be checking with you occasionally."

"Okay.—Esau, let's go get some coffee."

"Sure, sounds good."

The Sheriff put on his hat and they walked up to the restaurant.

"Esau, I guess you've got about everything pretty well taken care of."

"Yeah, I spoze so, Matt. Now, it's just sit back and see if everything comes together like planned.—You know, I'm not even sure yet, if she is coming. She might want to stay in the convent."

Matt saw the mental strain and worry in Esau's face as they went through the restaurant door. "Cheer up friend, I really don't think you have any worries. The wire from the Priest should do it. And, from what you've told me, there is no doubt that she loves you."

The waitress knew what they wanted, and set the coffee down as they sat down. "Now that is real service," said the

Sheriff. "Thank you, Agnes.—do you want something to eat, Esau."

"No, I better wait and eat at home, I don't want to get on Birdie's wrong side, she'll be expecting me to have supper."

"Yeah, best not to disappoint her."

"Where can I find a good haberdasher."

"What'cha gon'na buy?"

"A new hat."

"Ain't none here. There's a good one in Independence."

"Think I'll go find it tomorrow. I'll check in with'ya then."

Esau went home. He felt better after Birdie fed him.

A full week had elapsed when the wires started coming in. The first one made Esau jump with joy. Jose wired Sheriff Murdock that they would arrive in Kansas City on May fourteenth, at around noon. Three weeks away. The wire was short but the message was extremely long in happiness. Esau and Matt danced around the office and hugged each other while exclaiming loud intonations of jubilation.

He had bought himself a new hat, off white, narrower brim than his old hat. He had many compliments on it. He had the suit cleaned and pressed and was counting the days until his lovely nun would be home.

Could one be caught up in too much happiness all at once. Not Esau, a second wire came in the same day.

Esau, it said. "*Yes, the sorrel is yours. The carriage and team is in good condition, just needs cleaning. I have promised the liveryman three hundred for the lot. Bill is overjoyed. Carl Smith is on his way to the DBM to get the unmentionable and the Pinto He and Ed Trusdale will be here in three days to gear up and head for Kansas City. Wire me four hundred. Your friend Sam Logan."*

"I'm off to the Independence bank, Matt. I'll be back by."

In less than two hours Esau was instructing the bank to wire the Santa Fe bank eight hundred dollars for Marshall Sam Logan ; message, "more for the trip."

Esau's reasoning was a nice carriage for both church attendances, Catholic and Baptist. He knew all of the colored people attended a Baptist Church, They too, should go in style, and he wanted to give Carl Smith, *Smith, huh, I never knew his last name,* and Ed Trusdale a job if they needed one.

Esau stopped back in Blue Springs and went to have coffee with Matt. The young lady, Agnes, again brought the coffee as they sat down. Esau had never before noticed how pretty the lady was. He did notice intentionally that she did not have on a wedding band.

"Agnes," he asked. "Why is it, that such a beautiful young lady as yourself is not married?"

"Why, thank you for the compliment, Mister Jones. I am spoken for— it won't be long until we get married." She took the coffee pot back to the kitchen.

"What's a matter, Esau, you can't wait till your lady gets here."

"I was just being friendly Matt. I didn't mean nothing by it."

"I knew that. I was just being kind of impertinent."

"Naw you weren't. You thought I was trying to flirt with her." Esau grinned about it and told Matt that he was going on home and see what he could do constructive. They walked back to Matt's office, and Esau mounted the Bay and headed home.

As he unsaddled and put the Bay in the corral, Carlos approached him.

"Hey boss, I've been thinking about the stallion situation, and thought I might talk to you about it."

"What about it, Carlos?"

"Well boss, I know right now we are going to be pretty short on good stallions, what with Auggy bringing in a bunch of brood mares, and I wondered if you had a certain place where you would be looking for some."

"No, I've had my mind elsewhere. Do you have any ideas?"

"Yes Sir, that's why I brought it up. This time of the year, the Fort Worth stock barns will be selling and trading in young thoroughbreds of all kinds."

Esau looked thoughtfully toward Carlos while stroking his chin.

"I do really want to be here when my people from California arrive, but like you say, we will certainly need some stallions. Oh, I haven't told you , they will arrive in Kansas City on May the fourteenth. I better go tell Birdie and George."

"Our best chance in Fort Worth would be right now, sir."

"You go tell Lupe that you're leaving for a little while with me, and get your traveling gear and riding hoss. We will take the train. I'll be back to saddle the Bay directly. Maybe we can be back before they get here."

Esau went in and broke the news to Birdie and George, and told them to tell the staff. He told them he and Carlos were going after some stallions, and would be back, hopefully before Maria arrived. "If not, have Jim Conners to take the carriage and meet them at the train depot in Kansas City at noon on May the fourteenth."

"I'll go with him, Mister Jones." George said. "Just to be sure he don't forget what he's doing."

Esau grinned. "Okay George, that'll be great." He went upstairs and put on his old clothes which someone had washed and neatly folded. He adorned his old hat and put one of his pistols under his belt, picked up his saddle bags and went out through the back and found the Bay saddled, and Carlos ready to go. They stopped at the bank in Independence where Esau went in and drew out thirty thousand in one-thousand dollar bills and two thousand in one-hundred dollar bills.

Outside as he tied the saddlebags behind his saddle, he was listening to Carlos tell him that the Southern Pacific did not go straight down to Fort Worth. He said that they had to take the SP across Missouri to Saint Louis, and change to the SSW line which went south and veered across Arkansas and over to Fort Worth.

Once in Kansas City they went to the train depot, and Esau paid the fare for them and the horses all the way through the changeover and to Fort Worth as Carlos had explained. They were lucky to come when they did, as the train would be leaving in about two hours. They left the horses in the railroad holding corral, and with Esau's saddlebags slung across his left shoulder, they found a restaurant close by and had some supper. They returned to the depot in time to see their horses being loaded into the horse car, before settling down in the train for the ride across Missouri, where they would again watch their horses being unloaded and loaded into another train for the final, but longest leg to Fort Worth.

"Tell me something Carlos. Why is it you don't sound like a Mexican when you talk?"

"Well Sir, I've never even been in Mexico. I'm what you might call a Texas Mexican. I was raised in a small town between Houston and San Antonio. I went to school right along with regular Texas kids, and consequently I speak like a Texan."

"Ha, you never even been to Mexico."

"No Sir."

After making the changeover in Saint Louis, they settled down and slept through the night and half of the morning before disembarking the train in Houston and riding horseback for an hour to the horse corrals. They left their steeds at a holding area, and walked, with Esau's saddlebag over his shoulder, to the horse corrals. The corrals area was crowded with buyers and sellers. Carlos talked to some old acquaintances, before leading Esau to one particular corral of quarter horses. They saw two beautiful Red Roans, with splashes of yellow. A light tan Buckskin with Chestnut main and tail. A solid black Arabian. A blue grey Dun. Two red brown Bays. A beautiful golden yellow Palomino, with darker gold main and tail. A red with circled white running around the body, Choctaw Paint, similar to the Paint that Fred told him he cross-bred. What really caught Esau's eye was the motley blue and grey Appaloosa. There were also sorrels, but Esau dismissed the sorrels and Bays since he had one of each.

He had Carlos go inside the corral and check out each horse of interest to him. Carlos gave a thumbs up if he found the horse to be sound. He gave a thumbs down on one of the red Roans.

The seller was taking much interest in Esau and Carlos's activities, Esau turned to him.

"Sir, I'm interested in purchasing some of your hosses. They are for sale, are they not? My name is Esau Jones." He extended his hand. The man shook his hand and said his name was Tucker, and that he was a horse trader or seller, which ever struck the fancy. What horse do you think you're interested in."

"Not hoss, Sir, but hosses."

Tucker looked doubtfully at Esau. "Which ones are you interested in?"

"The red Roan with the brown halter on, the Buckskin, the black Arabian, the blue Dun, the Palomino, the Choctaw Paint, and the Appaloosa. That's seven hosses,— give me a price for the lot."

Tucker was flabbergasted, he stammered as he spoke. "Yes well, you do know that these horses are expensive, they go from six thousand each, with the Appaloosa running about ten."

"Let me tell you something Sir, I might have been born at night, but by God, it weren't last night. I'll give you four thousand each for seven, and an extra two on the Appaloosa. That's thirty thousand. I will expect a halter on each of them with seven twenty foot lengths of lasso rope."

Tucker noticed the pistol in Esau's waist band and hollowed for his men to cut out the horses that the Mexican points out to you. "Halter them and give them each a rope. They have been broke to the halter, Sir, and will lead good."

Esau paid Tucker the thirty thousand and got a receipt. He and Carlos took the horses and headed back to the train depot. With a big grin, Carlos told Esau he did well, and he surely liked his style of dealing.

Chapter 17

Upon arriving at the train depot and putting the horses in the railroad holding corral along with the Bay and Carlos's steed, they discovered that the train had three days or possibly more before departure. It was at this time being held up in Laredo, due to locomotive problems.

Esau and Carlos checked into a hotel near the depot to sit it out. With the stallions in tow, there was nothing they could do but wait and hope it would not take long to repair the locomotive. Days turned into weeks. One more day to the fourteenth. Maria would come in without him being there. Carlos consoled him.

"You know the house staff will welcome them in open arms. Everything will be just fine. It will give them time to get to know everyone and look the place over."

"I'd rather be there and let her look me over."

"Yes, I understand, I'd like to be with my Lupe, too. I'm sure we will be seeing them soon, Sir."

"They'll be in tomorrow, I hope Jim and George don't forget to pick them up."

"They want forget, Sir,—What say, let's take a walk and see how all those fine stallions are doing."

"You're just trying to get my mind off of my troubles, I know you by now."

"Yes Sir."

"Alright, let's go, I need to get out of this room. We can check again to see if the station manager has heard anything."

"Yes Sir."

Meanwhile, back at the farm, the next day.

Jim and George waited as the train came to a stop. All of the passengers unloaded. George spotted them on the platform and approached them as he gingerly gestured with his hand.

"Senor Jose, Senora Rosa, and Maria, I presume?"

"Yes," Jose answered.

"My name is George, I am your butler. The man behind me is Jim. He is one of the hands at the farm.—Well, I thought he was behind me. Anyway, we have come to take you home."

"Where is Esau?" Maria asked.

"He and one of the hands, Carlos Cadero, went to Houston to buy some stallions. They expected to be back before you got here. I'm sure they will be coming in most anytime. In the meantime you can get to know all of your servants and your cook at the house."

Jose, Rosa and Maria, looked disbelievingly at one another as Jim took their baggage down the ramp to the carriage.

"Where were you, Jim?"

"I went into the station to check on the train from Houston. It seems it has had engine problems and is held up in Laredo, for an undetermined amount of time."

As they got into the carriage, Rosa looked it over with admiring approval. "Does this fine carriage belong to Esau?"

"Oh, yes Mam."

"And the pretty horses?" Maria asked.

"Yes Mam, the farm and everything on it belongs to you and Mister Esau."

Jim drove the carriage as George pointed out different landmarks. He told them when they passed through Independence. He told them that they were in Jackson County where Esau was raised as a boy. He told them that Clay County was to the north where Esau's good friends, Jesse and Frank James live. When they entered Blue Springs, he told Jim to pull up to the bluff and let them see the Blue Springs Lake. He told them Esau always liked to stop and look out at it. He told them how Esau said it always made him feel relaxed to look at it. They sat and looked at the Lake for a few minutes before going on to the farm. When they pulled in to the archway, Jim stopped again and let them look at the home from a little distance. They were enchanted to the point of gawking instead of talking.

"When we get up to the house, me and Jim will take your bags in and introduce you to Birdie. She is your cook and pretty well runs the house. She will have some of the staff to show you your rooms. Now, you remember this is your home and they all work for you. So if you don't like your rooms, you just say so and find another one. Mister Esau's room is the Master bedroom. Have them to put Maria's bags in it."

Birdie was very discerning, and consequently very likeable. She told them about how all the servant's stayed on after the Emancipation Proclamation. And about how the Union Army confiscated all the horses, and about Bumgartner's wife passing away, and about him selling the farm to Esau.

"Listen now, if it's anything y'all folks want, just tell me and I'll do my best to get it. I normally cook southern soul food, but if'n ya'll want some Spanish food, with a little help, I'll fix it. Anything ya'lls heart desires between meals, just ring the little bell on the dining table and one of the servant's will come running."

As the days passed, Jose and Rosa felt like they had gone to Heaven. Jose found the books in the desk and studied how the farm had been run. He saw a few improvements he could institute. He also saw that the staff and hands had not been paid for two months. He would take care of that right away. He made arrangements for Jim to take him and Maria to the Independence Bank.

Maria had looked the entire place over except for the pasture land. She met and talked at length to the families in the section. She and Lupe had something in common. They missed their man and wanted them to come home. "Esau could probably fix the darn train if they would let him," she told Lupe. It at least gave them a laugh.

When Jim drove Jose and Maria to the Independence Bank, Jose told Maria that she had $200,000. in the Santa Fe Bank. He had not told her before, because he didn't want her to go off half cocked and maybe do something she would later regret. It was from what the Double-Bar-M had in the bank when they left and went to California. He had taken $10,000. For wages due him, which they traveled on to San Miguel. He still had most of it left. He wanted her to add her $200,000. to her and Esau's account. He told her he wanted to pay the back wages that the hands and servants had coming. "They are probably in need of personal items, and I have no idea of yours and his balance."

"Yes, by all means, let's put it in the bank and pay the staff and hands what they have coming."

"When they deposited the money by way of a money transfer from the Santa Fe Bank. It brought the balance in her and Esau's account up to $370,000. They both laughed about the worry, and she withdrew $2,000. in small bills for Jose to make the payroll. Jose had told her that the wages was twenty-five dollars per month for each person. That was pretty good he thought, considering housing and food was taken care of. He wanted to pay them all for the two back months. He would also have to pay Auggy when he arrived.

At this point in time, Carl and Ed had arrived in Tucumcari, and decided to see about the cost of taking the train. They needed four stalls in the horse car for the carriage team, the sorrel and the Pinto. They enlisted help in loading and securing the carriage on a flat car. With the seven-hundred dollars, they had ample money for the cost and their fare to Kansas City. So they would soon be surprising Maria, Jose and Rosa.

The combination of the D&RGW/SP/SSW railroad system finally got the train up from Laredo to Houston. The nine horses, including the Bay and Carlos's steed were loaded. Esau and Carlos were happy to listen to the clicking rails across Arkansas and up to Saint Louis where the changed trains, reloaded the horses and headed across the state on Southern Pacific to Kansas City.

Leading the seven stallions by haltered rope they headed toward Independence. About half way to Independence they encountered, in the road ahead of them, ten wranglers and

Auggy, driving a heard of forty-five mares and one solid white Arabian stud with black main and tail. Esau gave his lead ropes to Carlos and road up to the wranglers.

"Which one of you might be Auggy?"

"That would be me Sir," came the answer.

Esau rode up beside the man. "Auggy, my name is Esau Jones. Mister Bumgartner has returned to England. I bought the farm from him and plan on getting it back in full operating shape. So, to put it plainly, I'm the new boss. I will be keeping everyone on in their respective jobs.—Carlos and I are just returning from Houston with seven stallions. We're back a ways down the road. That is a damn nice white stallion you brought back. I bet it took all of the wranglers to break him."

"Yep, it sure did.—Soon as we get these mares inside, I'll come back and help y'all. I'm going to have to get some men to bring out the gate and put it back up. We took it down after the horses were gone. It's a gate that lifts up by balance weights, when you pull a rope."

"Great, I was wondering how we kept the hosses in."

"Mister Jones, I was going to ask Fred when we returned, so I will ask you. Can I get permission to build me a house down in the section. I've got myself engaged, and want to get married as soon as I have a place for her."

"Somebody you met in Wyoming?"

"No Sir, she lives in Blue Springs."

'You don't have time , right now, to be building a house Auggy. You show me where you want it and I'll have some builders to come in from Kansas City and construct it for you.—And by the way Auggy, you don't have to call me Mister, just plain Esau will do fine."

"Thank you very much Mis—Esau, I can't wait to tell Agnes."

"Would that be the Agnes at the restaurant?"

"Yes Sir.'

"Congratulations Auggy, she is an exceedingly lovely lady."

"Thank you."

"By the way Auggy, there will be two more hands coming in for'ya soon. They are bringing another two-up carriage with carriage hosses, and a most excellent sorrel stud, and my intended's Pinto. Their names are Carl Smith and Ed Trusdale. You can put them up in the bunkhouse."

Maria, Jose, Rosa and the entire house staff were standing outside the front watching the forty-five beautiful mares of all colors, run up the drive and cut out across the field into the pasture land. Auggy held on to the white stallion with a lead rope and took him around back and through the gate into the stallion acreage. He waved at everyone out front as he and the cowboys went by. He showed them the bunkhouse, and asked some of them to help him with the lift gate. They took it from the barn and out to the front where it was appropriately set up under the archway.

Esau and Carlos came in leading the stallions as the staff had turned and was going inside. Maria turned and looked back. She made a loud squealing exclamation, and began to run toward Esau. The others had turned when she squealed. They watched her with a feeling of great joy.

Esau gave the stallions and the Bay to Carlos, and ran to meet her. They embraced and kissed repeatedly. Nothing need be said. He lifted her in his arms and went through the front door and up the stairs, two steps at a time.

George, with a grin on his face, put his chair at the bottom of the stairs and declared the upstairs was off limits for the day.

Maria was moist even before reaching the stairs. Esau threw the cover back from the bed and pulled her down with him. She came willingly, still locked in his kiss. They clung to each other experiencing a strong desire of overpowering eroticism. Maria said nothing. Nor did he. Before even they were joined in love, he stripped away some of their clothing. She took the rest from him and herself. He entered her and they were one body, one will, as they slowly climbed the licentious stairway of eroticism, and lingered on the crest, daring not to fall. Inevitability, not to be denied, there occured a duel climax and they drifted amorously down to a gratifying absoluteness.

Maria lay limp under Esau's body in a semi-transfixed state of rapture with an unknowing smile on her face. Esau arose and had a cup of water while he looked at her sensuously gorgeous body. *"What have I ever done,"* he thought, *"for God to be this good to me."*

When Maria awoke, Esau was sitting on the side of the bed. She pulled him down to her, and soon they were climbing that stairway once again.

It is the contention of this writer that true love between a man and woman has always begun with a bit of unadulterated Lust.

The End

About the Author

Jim Feazell—Retired filmmaker and singer/songwriter worked in Hollywood for 22 years as a motion picture stunt actor and cinematographer, and also performed in folk clubs and coffeehouses as a singer.

After retiring from 17 years of stunt work he headed his own film company for fifteen years in Hollywood, Ca. El Dorado, Ar. and Tucson. Az. As a member of Writer's Guild of America West, he wrote and sold numerous highly acclaimed screenplays, ie; A Deadly Obsession, Two Guns to Timberline, Redneck Mama, and others. Jim wrote, produced and directed the theatrical cult movie, Wheeler, aka Psycho from Texas.

In his twilight years, Jim has become a novelist. This book, "Esau Jones, bounty hunter" is his eighth book.